A
SEED ONCE
SOWN

A SEED ONCE SOWN

JESSICA RANEY

Cursed Dragon Ship
PUBLISHING

Copyright © 2023 by Misplaced Adventures

Cursed Dragon Ship Publishing, LLC

6046 FM 2920 Rd, #231, Spring, TX 77379

captwyvern@curseddragonship.com

Cover © 2023 by We Got You Covered Book Design

Developmental Edit by Jesse Sprague

Proofread by Kelly Lynn Colby

ISBN 978-1-951445-52-2

ISBN 978-1-951445-53-9 (ebook)

This book is a work of fiction fresh from the author's imagination. Any resemblance to actual persons or places is mere coincidence.

Lonely Bay

The Troll Coast

Tower of Chains

Bitter Heights Mountains

Goldspine

The Deathless Tundra

Brittlepin

Blackwood River

Greenmire

Greenshade River

Orad

The Paxas Plains

...shade

Lav'alar

Shadow

Helshai

Daggerune

...Old Oak

Grasshouse

Treaty Hill

Three Sisters Wood

Oulan

Banah'sek

Ghazmin

Sailing

Red River

Agran-ti

Bright Morning Bay

The Beacon Sea

Ippem

Stonewood

Ghamin'

Kos

Okkan

Daunce

Verran

The Breadbelt

Foul Hill

Vastard

Middlefield

Egren

Green Serpent River

Weslh

Deep Knotting

The Yellow Sea

Poll's

Weatley

Plensa

Wearbrey

Darkfen Marsh

Ardin

Farpond

Breach

For all the girls who wanted swords instead of dolls.

CHAPTER
ONE

The shimmering cobalt-blue blade sliced so easily through the man's neck that Mags barely felt the blade slow. As his head landed in the dirt road with a thud and a poof of dust, Mags held the blade up to the light. The weapon's elegant curve—the shape of a simple sickle used to harvest grain—merged seamlessly with the flesh of Mag's forearm, an impossible physical extension of herself that even in three hundred years Mags had never really gotten used to wielding. The weapon vibrated and she felt the trickle of blood that remained on the blade, thick and wet, as if it were on her own fingers and a pleasant tingle that radiated down the blade and into her body. All of it was short-lived as any wonder she may have had at the simple beauty of the blade and the magic that made it a part of her disappeared when the pain came.

Mags threw her head back and screamed. Both the flesh and the metal glowed, dark red at first, then as the temperature rose to the heat of a well-stoked blacksmith's forge, they glowed a bright golden yellow, the color of butter. It was an impossibility for the flesh of a human to withstand forge welding temperatures, and yet Mags's arm didn't char. As it glowed, the blade began to shrink and the metal moved in reverse. With every inch it receded inside Mags's arm, it spit and sizzled, and Mags screamed.

Finally, the blade was gone and only Mag's left hand remained. Shrunken and cramped, it still glowed yellow, but it quickly cooled to a dull red, then back to its normal color—a deep cobalt blue. Her fingers remained curled in a claw shape. Unable to move them, Mags fell to her knees and the world spun as every muscle in her body seized.

She fell to her knees close to the man's head. His dead eyes, wide open and full of fear and surprise, stared up at her. She cramped again, then collapsed in the road and rolled over onto her back. The mid-day sun blazed down on her. A breeze blew in and rustled through the trees that lined the road. As Mags stared up at the leaves, she blinked her eyes. Her vision returned to normal from the red-tinted view it was when she had the scent of a soul and the leaves looked green again. The red mark on her cheek burned one last time, a match struck, then it faded to a sting like a bad sunburn.

Mags writhed in the dirt. Her hand still burned and her muscles spasmed every few seconds. The pain was excruciating, but after nine hundred and ninety-nine harvests she was able to manage the pain. That was easy. It was what would come next that she dreaded.

She closed her eyes and concentrated on the chirping birds and the rustling of the leaves. She let the familiar sounds of nature—her favorite thing—calm and distract her from the pain and her heaving chest. The little sparrows in the elm tree above her sang their happy little song. Mags smiled as she listened to them chirp at one another and imagined they were two old friends sharing the gossip of the day. Her smile faded as the voices drifted in on the breeze and drowned out the gossip of the songbirds.

At first they were simply whispers, light and unintelligible, but gradually they grew louder, bolder, and meaner.

"Murderer . . ."

"Evil . . ."

"Monster . . ."

Mags squeezed her eyes shut and gritted her teeth as she tried to ignore them. She desperately trained her ear on the birds, but to no avail. Nine hundred and ninety-nine voices all demanded her attention and they would have it. Mags shook and huddled in the dirt as they escalated to screaming. She couldn't make out what any of them were saying. All she could do was lay there and bear the brunt of their verbal assault as they aired their anger, fear, and frustration.

"My crops . . ."

"I was so young . . ."

"Who will take care of my children . . ."

After a bit, the screams diminished and faded back to whispers. Tears ran down Mags's cheeks as what came next was worse than any physical pain she endured and more awful than the litany of angry voices she weathered. Her eyes felt heavy and so did all her bones as a wave of exhaustion washed over her. She fought against the sleep, kicking and twitching in the dirt like a toddler fighting a nap, but no amount of fighting would stop it. She would fall asleep, which happened very rarely. In fact, it only happened right after a Harvest. For that, she was always grateful because when the sleep came it brought the dreams with it, and in those dreams she relived every Harvest, and saw every head the cobalt-blue blade took. She had to answer to every soul she had taken in the name of Kohoc the Harvester—nine hundred and ninety-nine of them now, each one angry, confused and terrified. Each one demanded answers from Mags, and in every single case, in every single dream, she had none to give.

WHEN MAGS WOKE up she was sore but the pain in her hand was nearly gone. She tried to flex it, but it was still a misshapen claw. Even so, she was able to wiggle her fingers as she sat up. The hand ached, but it had ever since Matchi the Huntress had taken Kohoc the Harvester's weapon and grafted it to her arm. The dark blue color had faded to a light blue tint. It still contrasted with her olive skin, but it was less noticeable than before.

Mags blinked. Her vision was normal. The red haze that colored her view while she was harvesting a soul was gone. But the sleep had done nothing to quell her exhaustion—it never did. Her heart beat steady in her chest with just a hint of a second beat. Half of her heart belonged to another creature, one of Matchi's hounds, and she never stopped feeling a strange flutter as it beat, the hound half ever so slightly out of sync with the human half. The other half Matchi had shoved into the chest of the hound itself so somewhere that animal felt the same. Mags took comfort in that and at the same time felt guilty. Sometimes it seemed like everyone was caught between the Huntress and the Harvester. It was not a good place to be.

She scanned the sky and let out an exasperated sigh. The sun had sunk a quarter of the way across the horizon and the way the light glowed and bounced off the terrain told her it was late afternoon. Mags stood up and dusted herself off. Her clothes were free of blood and there was no blood anywhere to be found on the road or anywhere else. The man she had beheaded sat in the road, slumped against his hand cart. His head was attached and his eyes were closed. Anyone who came upon him now would observe a tired man who had died pulling his vegetable cart to a market day somewhere along the Summer Trades. Mags knelt beside him and paused for a moment.

"I hope your life was full and I hope now you're at peace," she said.

This was the nine hundred and ninety-ninth time she had

harvested a soul. She only had one more to go to fulfill her debt to the Harvester. She briefly thought she ought to feel happy about it, happy that her three-hundred-year torment was nearly over. But she didn't feel any semblance of happiness, or even relief. All she thought of was the next Harvest to come. With every one of them, she hoped that the sadness, regret, and revulsion at what she had done would lessen, but it never had.

The nine hundred and ninety-ninth was, if anything, more painful, her sadness greater, and her revulsion nearly unbearable. Thinking of what the thousandth would feel like made her ill. Bile surged up her throat and she swallowed it down, then spat into the dirt to clear her mouth. The man had several waterskins hanging from his cart, but Mags left them alone. She had already taken enough from him and she wouldn't take any more, not even a sip of water.

"I'm sorry," she said.

The words seemed inadequate, but all words were. She knew. She'd said them often enough.

Mags stood up, pushed down all her feelings, and looked around to determine where she had ended up. She didn't recognize it, but she didn't need to. When she turned her body in the direction she had come, something akin to the smell of a campfire, smokey and pleasant, came to her nose. It wasn't a real fire, but it was a smell she liked and it was always what led her back.

As the sun sank lower toward the horizon, Mags set off, following the smell. Her own footprints in the deep dust of the road confirmed that she was headed back the way she had come. She sucked in a big breath, then increased her pace to a steady jog. If she was lucky, she hadn't run too far from her camp and if she was very, very lucky, her knots had held and her bounty was still tied up and waiting.

In over three hundred years, Mags had never, ever been that lucky.

CHAPTER
TWO

Mags ran all night and arrived at her camp just as the sun peeked over the horizon, bathing the campsite and surrounding forest in red and gold. The new daylight sparkled off the dew and spiderwebs, and the little birds chirped and sang as they welcomed the day. All of this beauty and natural music was lost on Mags at the moment. Her bounty, Bog, was gone.

"Bukker's Seventh Cock!" she yelled. She had tied him up well and the ropes were strong, but Bog had found a rock sharp enough to saw through them. The rope lay next to the rock. The ends were dark and frayed and smelled burnt. She hadn't really given Bog that much credit for intelligence or perseverance, but she supposed even a blind squirrel found a nut every once in a while. He had certainly had the benefit of plenty of time.

The campfire was cold. Her gear remained. She carried two fighting batons in holsters on her belt as well as several throwing knives and a long knife that was multi-purposed but could be used in a fight. Mags preferred her batons. In the hands of someone who knew how to use them, they were fast, light, and devastating when trying to disable someone. Mags didn't

6

carry a sword. She liked to avoid deadly force when she could, and anyway, swords reminded her of her hand, the deadly gift from Kohoc the Harvester and Matchi the Huntress. A tool to be used to serve them both. Mags hated to be reminded of it.

The fact that she had her weapons and gear was good, at least Bog had been in a hurry and hadn't stolen anything she actually needed at the moment. Her saddlebags were turned out though and her coin purse was gone. Mags shook her head and closed her eyes. It was unfortunate but not desperate. She could always make more money. Bounties were plentiful, especially in these times right after the wars as everyone tried to restore balance and order to their areas. They weren't necessarily big paydays, but Mags preferred steady money to windfalls and easy bounties to difficult ones. Her personal needs were small and bounties filled in the time between Harvests as well as allowed her to move around. Staying in one place too long wasn't good. She made people nervous. Even if they didn't know her as the Hound of Matchi, the Huntress, which was terrifying enough, the fact that she was an agent of Kohoc the Harvester, Death himself, cast an aura of dread around her that everyone from The Lonely Bay to The Paradisals could feel, even if they didn't know what to attribute it to.

Life was much easier for her on the move and unattached to people. She had many acquaintances. Three hundred years was a long time and even though she tried to limit her contact with people, her job and if she were honest with herself—which she seldom was—her personality, made avoiding people difficult if not impossible. Still, she eschewed any partners even though many in her profession often worked together for safety and to collect more dangerous and profitable bounties. To Mags, partners complicated matters and they led to attachment. And to someone who had been alive for many lifetimes of man, attachment was painful and dangerous.

Mags allowed herself companions though. Her two horses,

massive, solid animals named Duck and Goose grazed peacefully at the grass around the perimeter of the camp. They raised their heads and nickered at her in greeting, then went back to eating. Well-trained and even-tempered, Duck and Goose would wait for her for as long as it took her to get back to them.

She followed Bog's footprints to the place where she had bedded down the horses the night before. She found Duck's track and bent down to look at it closely. One of his back tracks was deeply cut into the dirt, indicating the big war horse had reared up and put all his weight on his back legs. Mags laughed when she found a man-shaped place in the dirt. Bog had tried to steal Duck, but the horse had thrown him.

"Nice work, Duck," Mags said to the animal. The big black horse plodded over, whinnied at her, then bumped her with his forehead. She petted him and scratched his ears.

"I bet he enjoyed that ride."

The horse nodded his head up and down and nickered at her in an affirmative. Mags grinned at him, hugged his neck, and gave him a final pat.

Goose wandered over and demanded attention as well. A full hand height bigger than Duck, Goose stood eighteen hands high, and where Duck was black with black mane and forelock, Goose was a deep chestnut with a white mane and socks. He was slightly more patient than Duck, so she usually put the bounties on Goose and she rode Duck. But every once in a while she switched it up lest he think she played favorites. Both animals were attuned to her. She spoke to them like they were humans and equals, and to Mags, they were. When she hurt, they knew, and after a Harvest, they always knew.

Mags had a way with animals and all her horses, there had been several, were wonderful companions, but as she neared closer to the one thousandth soul, she got edgier with the prospect of her own death and the consequences of her lifetimes of harvesting. Her anxiety didn't faze Duck or Goose. The big animals doubled down in love and patience. They soothed her nerves and never wavered in devotion.

Goose whinnied at her and bumped her with his forehead, then he leaned against her. Mags smiled at the contact and leaned into the big animal's warm body. She hugged him. "Yes. It wasn't as long this time. But I guess it was long enough for that idiot to escape."

The horses nickered in unison.

Mags patted them both, then looked around the camp a bit more. Bog's tracks led off in the direction of the nearest town, Skiffton. On the one hand, Bog making for Skiffton made things easy. He wasn't one to blend in. He was loud and obnoxious, which was why she had found him so easily to start with. He wasn't smart enough to cover his tracks either.

Mags sighed and winced as she flexed her healing hand. While catching up to him was simple enough, which was a good thing, his predictable stupidity bored her. In three hundred years, it didn't seem like people had gotten any smarter, especially not mediocre criminals like Bog. Sometimes she wished for a bit more of a challenge. But bounty hunting was nothing if not consistent in its proximity to predictable stupidity. At least it kept her in horse feed, even if it did add to her general malaise.

Mags shook off her bored annoyance because an easy snatch of Bog was preferable to some genius plan of his. And anyway, she needed the coin. She saddled the horses and cleared up the camp. She worked efficiently but didn't rush. There was no need. If Bog was in Skiffton, there was only one place he would go and he'd be there a while. She mounted Duck and headed off toward Skiffton, confident that Bog would be in a place almost identical to the one in which she had found him—a brothel.

CHAPTER
THREE

Mags arrived in Skiffton at mid-day. It had always been a good-sized town, on the northern reach of the Trades, Mirrik, but not Norrik, with the typical bravado of the region tempered partly by the exposure to trade and travel.

War had helped too. It tended to inspire movement. The town bustled with wagons and carts transporting goods and people around. Commerce and refugees were the natural progressions of most wars. The taverns and brothel appeared to be doing brisk business even so early. Located squarely in the center of town, The Blue Fox's classy name belied its purpose. Although for a brothel, it was quite nice. Mags had seen a lot of brothels in her time, as the people she was most often looking for gravitated toward the establishments. As a result, Mags knew a lot of tavern keepers and brothel owners, and while she couldn't say she counted all of them as friends, she could say she was friendly with more of them than she wasn't. And in the first bit of luck she'd had in a few days, the proprietress of the Blue Fox, Andie Tavers, had been a friend for nearly thirty years.

When Mags walked in, Andie was at the bar. She grinned at

Mags and Mags grinned back as she sat down. Andie put a cup of red wine in front of her old friend.

"Magdalena, my darlin'. It's been a long time."

"Has it?" Mags asked. It didn't seem to her like it had been that long, but she had to admit that judging periods of time wasn't her strong suit.

"It's been at least ten years," Andie said. "But I guess that doesn't mean much in your world."

Mags shrugged. "Long is long." She glanced about the place as she sipped her wine. It was only mid-morning so the place was quiet. The Fox did brisk business in the evenings but during the day, the girls did odd jobs, sewing, washing, normal types of work. Mags had always found that amusing, but Andie was a shrewd businesswoman and liked steady money coming in. She despised idleness.

Of course, the girls were all different, which was to be expected, and the place a little worn, but it was clean. Andie ran a tight ship, no nonsense. Even in her middle age, she was still a beautiful woman. Her hair, once the shade of mid-summer hay, had faded to gray, but her beautiful brown eyes were warm. They sparkled with happiness and mischief. She sat down next to Mags and sipped her own wine. She patted Mags on the knee.

Mags put her hand on Andie's and squeezed it. "How's business, Andie?"

"Better than it has been, not as good as it once was. War takes a toll, changes things. You working?"

"Aren't I always?" Mags didn't see Bog anywhere but that didn't mean he wasn't there. "I'm looking for a skinny ratface. Fancy mustache."

Andie nodded and laughed. "Oh yes. He came in last night. A real mouthy one. He bragged all over about robbing you and escaping."

"I suppose he did do those two things."

"He was with Big Rosie. Threw your coin all around."

"Well, at least my coin went to you." Mags smiled and winked at her friend as she saluted her with the cup of wine. "Is he upstairs?"

"He surely is. I told Rosie to wear him out for you."

Mags laughed and finished her wine. "I'll tip her proper."

"Just out of curiosity, Magdalena, how did an idiot like that get away from you?"

"Well. You know." Mags held up her hand. It was healing and more functional, but still not whole.

Andie's face reddened and she quickly changed the subject before Mags could reference her harvest. Even her long-time friends had difficulty with it. She didn't blame them. It made her a monster.

"What did he do?"

"He owes money in Deep Knotting."

Andie refilled the wine cups. "That's a long way. They should double his bounty for having to go that far with such a mouthy cuss."

Mags nodded. "Yeah. But that's the job. I take what I can get. I accepted the contract. I have no choice but to deliver him."

"I think you're the only one who follows that code nowadays. But then you've always been one to make things more difficult on yourself." Andie laughed. "He said he shanked you and tied you up. We had a chuckle at that. I was hoping you'd be quick about tracking him so I could watch you nab him."

"It didn't take much skill. I found him in a brothel in Bally Fjord. I have now found him in a brothel in Skiffton. People are nothing if not predictable," Mags said.

"That's true," Andie agreed. "But, Magdalena, you're one of the only trackers I know who doesn't have a partner. Somebody to watch their back. Don't you think that would make these things easier?"

Mags grimaced. "Not this shit again, Andie. We've been

down this road before. Partners . . . me . . . that's a problem for many reasons."

"Yes, I know. You've said. Attachment. Aging."

"Don't forget the backstabbing," Mags said. "The inevitable double-cross."

"Don't be so cynical. Not everyone will cross you."

"Oh really? From you?" Mags laughed and gestured around the brothel. "You see it all. All day. Every day. Are you really going to sit there and tell me people are trustworthy? You? Remember Raoul?"

"He was Tyrranean. That doesn't count."

"If you say so." Mags laughed and took another drink of wine. "But I seem to recall you were a bit more worked up when I brought him back to you. Worked up enough to cut off his—"

Andie cut her off. "What's passed is passed, Magdalena. Don't change the subject. Your life might be a little less misery if you'd at least go in with a business partner." She waived her hand and flipped it at Mags. "I'm not even talking about a romance. I know that's a lost cause. Not even Matchi The Huntress could find that for you."

"Don't even mention her name," Mags said. "That's the last thing I need right now. Look, betrayal aside, there is the dying part that's not good. Partners die. I don't."

At that, Andie shut up. She couldn't counter that. When they had met, Andie had been a girl of eighteen. Thirty years later, she was older and she looked it. Mags still looked twenty. She didn't age at all. Her black hair still shone bright, not a hint of gray in it and her face was smooth and unlined, just as it had been when she'd come into the service of Matchi and Kohoc. Her friends' hair grew thin and gray, their skin wrinkled, and their backs bent. Mags was still fit and tall, even if she did feel every bit of her age and the weight of her work.

It had been that way with so many friends Mags had lost count. They aged and died. She didn't. At least not on the outside. Losing them was hard. They didn't ever seem to understand that. None of them. And what's more, none of them understood the finality approaching her as she neared her thousandth soul. Mags couldn't blame them for that. People never understood finality for themselves either. And they certainly couldn't comprehend facing those thousand souls and their anger and fear and sadness for her own eternity. That dark cloud hung over Mags, ever warring with exhaustion and loss. Her good friends could feel it, even if they couldn't understand it. Andie was one of those good friends.

She gave Mags a genuine smile and patted her knee one last time. "Well, last door on the left." Andie finished her wine, stood up and went behind the bar.

Mags gulped down the last of her drink. She followed Andie behind the bar and gave the woman a hug. "Ten years was too long. I should make it back this way more often."

Andie hugged her tightly. "Your friends worry about you, Magdalena. Dying's not the worst thing in this life. Not even close. You know that better than anyone."

Mags smiled and kissed the woman on the cheek. "Truer words were never spoken." She kissed the other cheek, then winked and kissed Andie square on the lips. "Take care of yourself."

"Learn to let someone take care of you."

"That job is thankless, and the pay is shit." Mags laughed and started up the stairs.

Big Rosie had been there the last time Mags had passed through. She was at least six and a half feet tall and solid. If Big Rosie didn't want to move, she didn't. If Big Rosie wanted you to move, it really didn't matter what you wanted. She functioned as a sort of bouncer for the brothel, although Andie seldom required the assistance. Rosie sat at her vanity, picking at a dry place on her chin. She was wearing a silk robe that was too short for her. Fortunately, Mags wasn't shy. Bog was sound asleep on the bed. Rosie had hog-tied him.

"Hello, Rosie."

"How far you gotta take this one, Mags?"

"Deep Knotting."

"Ask double. He's awful."

"Oh, I know. Thanks for detaining him for me." Mags examined Bog's bonds. "I hope he appreciated your artistry with a knot."

"Seems like he wouldn't be able to get the drop on you. You're slipping, Magdalena."

"Oh, you have no idea." Mags dug in her pocket and pulled out a copper coin. She flipped it to Rosie. "Where's his clothes?"

Rosie held up a bundle of clothes. "I had them washed."

Mags tossed her another coin. "He was ripe. That's another favor I owe you."

"We're even. I won't forget that time you helped me with that fella from Kos." Big Rosie might have been grateful for the long-ago favor, but she was still a businesswoman. She kept the coins.

Mags saluted her and took the bundle of clothes. "What did you give him?"

"Valerian. I didn't think it would knock him out this long. I was worried for a minute I might have kilt him."

"He's slight, that's a fact," Mags said. Bog was skinny. If he weighed a third of what Big Rosie weighed, she'd have been shocked. "Well, it's good for me. Although I kind of wish he had pants on." Mags grimaced as she hefted Bog and slung him across her shoulder. He mumbled and flopped around, all of him, as she shifted him into a manageable carrying position.

"Can't win them all, Mags," Big Rosie said as she went back to her vanity.

Mags gave her a quick peck on the cheek as she carried Bog out. "Nope, you sure can't."

Andie followed her outside to the horses. Mags slung Bog across Goose's saddle and tied him so he wouldn't fall off. His bony, bare ass jutted to the sky. He grumbled unintelligibly and looked around with cloudy eyes as she finished up, but then collapsed against the saddle.

"I hope this is the last trouble you see for a bit, Magdalena," Andie said. She crossed her arms and pulled her shawl around her shoulders.

Mags mounted Duck and laughed out loud. "No trouble? For me? That's the only impossible thing there is."

She waved at Andie as she headed the horses out of town.

FOUR

If you kick that horse again, you won't be riding and it's a long way to Deep Knotting."

Mag's tone wasn't exactly conversational, but it was calm, possibly even pleasant, yet the delivery somehow managed to convey the threat. Bog had finally woken from his forced nap grumpy and spouting many colorful curses at her both for finding him again and his lack of pants. Even so, Mags kindly allowed him to get dressed before she tied him up again and they resumed their trek. He repaid the kindness with non-stop bitching and kicking of his mount. The bitching she could take, but never would Mags allow anyone to abuse her horses.

She stopped Duck and let Goose pull even with them. Both animals were so well-trained that no matter how hard Bog kicked, neither would go any faster or any place Mags didn't direct them. Still, Bog struggled. He worked to untie his hands and kicked his mount to spur him forward. Goose turned his head and laid his ears back. Mags dismounted and soothed him. He pressed his big head to her chest, and she scratched him behind his ear in the place he liked. Then she turned her attention to the grubby, rat-faced man. She smiled at him. He spat at her, then kicked Goose again.

Mags yanked him from the saddle and threw him to the ground. The force knocked the breath from him, and he rolled over and clutched at his chest as he struggled to breathe. Mags put a knee to his chest, grabbed his greasy hair, and punched him squarely in the nose. It crunched and squelched at the same time—a satisfying and just sound—then exploded in a bloom of red as blood gushed from it. She grabbed his hair again and held him still.

"Riding is a privilege. If you can't do it properly, you can walk."

"Why should I give a fiddler's fart about your beast?"

"You know, Bog, the bounty on you is more with you alive, but I'll be fine with half the value for just your head." Mags smiled at him and tilted her head as his eyes widened. "What do you think, Goose? Would you prefer just his head?"

The big horse stomped his foreleg and nodded. Duck did the same in agreement. Mags looked down at the bloody mess that was Bog and shrugged. "They're fine with half-pay."

Bog whimpered and clutched at his ruined nose as he scooted away and shook his head. Mags held up her blue hand and wiggled her fingers. She began chanting nonsense. Nothing she said or did would make the hand change into the weapon. That was for the gods to order, and she couldn't affect it all. But what Bog didn't know wouldn't hurt him and would certainly benefit her. She smiled as she approached the terrified man. He panicked and screamed as he scrambled in the dirt, unable to find his feet. Mags was on him quickly, and she planted a boot on the side of his head, pinning him to the ground. She closed her eyes and mumbled the fake incantation again.

"Please. No. Not that. Not that."

Mags nodded. "You're right. This blade isn't for you, but if you kick my horse again, it will be. Do you understand me?" She stepped harder on his face.

"I won't kick him no more."

"Excellent. He'll be happy to hear it, and I'll be happier with full price." She pulled Bog to his feet. The sun dipped lower on the horizon and the distance from the hills ahead told her they had only a few hours of daylight left.

If they followed the Summer Trades, they'd hit the fork and from there it was an easier trip to the inland Beacon Sea. The further she got from Tyrrane the better. In fact, the further she got from the North in general, the better. It wasn't just the cold; she'd never really understood the Andosh and if she lived another three hundred years, she still wouldn't. The world liked to talk about the snobbery of the Darrish, and that certainly was a thing, but that was a show, a dance of custom and bluster. It was annoying, but manageable. Dealing with the Norrikmen and the Mirrikmen, or worse, the Tyrraneans was a constant slogging fight over nothing. It was exhausting. But a job was a job and bounties were honest work, better than most alternative forms of employment, even when it took her to the giant, frozen asshole that was the North.

They were currently in Mirrik. It wasn't exactly the gentlest of places, but it wasn't inhospitable either. It would be safe enough to find a spot to camp. The forest that bordered the road wasn't wild and overgrown. She grabbed Bog and dragged him along with her. The horses followed. She found a clearing next to a stream about fifty yards off the road. It showed signs of heavy use with a burned-out fire circle and tamped down earth where travelers had spread bedrolls. Mags didn't like it. Too predictable, too easy for others to stumble upon them. She didn't need any more complications.

She headed down the stream a bit, maybe fifty yards from the original spot where a gigantic, gnarled oak stood sentinel next to the stream. Its huge roots made a natural dugout shelter and provided camouflage from other travelers. She could have a small fire and it wouldn't be seen by the other camp or by anyone on the road.

She shoved Bog down and he nestled into a tree root, scooting as far away from her as he could get. Mags pulled a small length of rope from Goose's saddle bag. She hobbled the man, then threw him a water bag. Bog fumbled at it, but finally opened it and drank greedily. Mags tossed him a rag and he dabbed at his bloody, broken nose, cursing her under his breath, but too afraid of her to do it proper loud. She ignored him and set about taking care of the horses.

It was her favorite part of the day. She unbuckled their saddles and removed the pads, then she massaged them and rubbed them down all over with a soft cloth. The smooth strokes across their slick coats calmed her. As she brushed them down she sang to them. When their coats were shiny perfection, she led them to the stream for water, then fed them from their grain bags. Only when the two animals were calm and content did Mags make a fire and grab a piece of jerky from her bag. She sat down opposite Bog.

He looked longingly at the jerky. "Can't I get none? I'm hungry," Bog complained.

"Supper is for people who don't mistreat horses." Both of the horses nickered, and Mags saluted him with the jerky.

Darkness had fallen and the small, economical fire crackled and warmed the hollowed-out area where they camped. Mags tied Bog securely to the tree and gagged him. "Bedtime for you. Keep quiet and still and maybe you'll get to ride in the morning instead of walk."

He cursed at her through his gag, but Mags patted him on the head, then settled in across the fire from him. She stared into the flames. Mags tuned out the crackle of the fire and the normal background noise of the woods. The normal night noises —insects and little creatures were absent, the chilly night sending them deep into holes and hollows, so when she heard the snap of twigs and the rustle of brush, she listened closer, knowing instinctively that it wasn't mundane.

She detected three distinct sounds. One of them was big. Their movements were clumsy, and Mags visualized a broad-shouldered hulk doing their best to move smoothly and quietly through the terrain and failing miserably as their bulk was just too large to be stealthy. The second was a much smaller person. Their noise came from careless steps and fast-talking whispers that carried longer and louder than a voice at normal volume. The third was trickier. They moved quietly and carefully but stopped every so often and shushed the fast whisperer, annoyed.

She smiled. They were just kids, idiots. She didn't need to see them to know it. They stopped about twenty yards out and argued. The fast talker wanted to rush in, the big one wanted to go home, and the third stayed quiet, but Mags knew they won the argument, because they all moved back to the well-used camp. They weren't trying to be quiet any longer and they built a large fire. The snap and crackle of it rang out through the night. As Mags listened to them, she closed her eyes for just a second and when she did, she heard a loud whisper that shocked her out of her relaxed state and made her jump so that she nearly fell into the campfire.

"No."

Mags looked all around and then down at her hand. It was nearly healed and light blue. She flexed it and felt no pain, no burning. When she reached up to touch the mark on her cheek, it was cool. There was no Harvest.

Her heartbeat calmed and she listened closely, but the whisper was gone. The only things she could hear were the crackle of the campfires and the sounds of the idiots in the big camp as they argued amongst themselves. Mags shrugged to herself and settled back against the tree root to do what passed for sleep for her, which was to close her eyes and wish she could remember what real rest felt like.

CHAPTER
FIVE

Mags nudged Bog awake with the toe of her boot after she'd groomed and saddled the horses. She removed his gag and hobble. "Just remember, Bog, this gag can go back on at any time. And if that doesn't work, your bounty is the same whether you have a tongue or not," Mags said.

Bog scowled at her but nodded. He understood.

Mags whistled to Duck and Goose and everyone walked back toward the community camp. Mags paused there and read the signs. Three sets of prints littered the camp confirming her assessment from the night before. As she knelt and examined the tracks, she began to get a clear sense of the party.

One set was made by a large man. His track was nearly double her own and set deep in the damp dirt, indicating his heavy steps. The other two sets told her one was a small person, short and slight. The footprint was as slender as a woman's, but their spacing and depth suggested to her that they belonged to a man. His steps flittered and shuffled about the camp and he had tossed and turned in place as he had slept, close to the fire. The third's track was hardest to pick up, but it was also small. The third person had been more intentional about where they stepped and hadn't slept much. Their space near the fire was back against the large log that ringed the site and Mags pressed her hand in the indentation where they had sat all night rather than reclined.

The fire bed was still warm. She'd heard them move out just before sunrise. They'd been only slightly stealthier in the pale light. Mags frowned. She still had the feeling they were very young and also idiots, but their purposeful early rise suggested they had some kind of plan. If there was one thing that Mags knew, it was that the plans of idiots were messy and inconvenient.

"No."

Mags jumped again when the voice rang louder in her ears this time. She looked to Bog, but he only yawned. He hadn't heard it. Mags shook her head and calmed herself. Disembodied voices were an unwelcome addition to her life, but as someone who regularly had strange and impossible things happen to them, Mags did her best to move on. She would know what the voice wanted when she knew. That was all there was to that.

She helped Bog onto Goose and gave him a mirthless smile. "Last chance to behave, Bog." She handed him a piece of jerky, which he devoured, then she mounted Duck, and they plodded back to the road.

They made steady progress until mid-day. She stopped to rest the horses and examined the tracks in the road. The trio of idiots had been ahead of them all morning; they'd made no attempt to disguise their tracks, but at some point, the tracks disappeared from the road. A quick look into the brush told Mags that the three had moved off, but quickened pace to get further ahead. Mags smelled ambush. She scowled. It had been a pain to track down Bog. He was a pain to transport, and she had a long way to go before payout. Again, the careful plans of morons were messy and inconvenient.

She wondered what it would be. The terrain wasn't particularly conducive to an ambush—the hills were rolling and the trail wide. The best way would be to block the road and force them to funnel into a congested area. Mags almost laughed out loud when she saw them.

The big kid lay in the middle of the road. The fidgety one danced around him in a fake panic, frantically and over-dramatically waving her down to help. Both looked to be eighteen or nineteen. Adults, yet not quite. The third wasn't in the road, but was likely behind Mags, waiting to jump her.

"Thank Oldam and blessings from above! My friend. He-he fell and I've no idea what to do!" The skinny kid hopped like a flea around the prone body of the big guy. He was the fast whisperer and looked exactly like Mags had pictured him—small, slight, and over-confident in his clever ruse.

The horses snorted and eyed him. Mags didn't dismount. She smiled down at the Flea.

"Try some water." She tossed him a water skin. The Flea caught it but didn't move to give any to his companion.

"I tried that already. He's dying! Please? Won't you help us?"

"I'm afraid I'm not a healer, friend. If water doesn't work, all I can offer is to ride ahead to Markton and send help back."

"Markton? Why, Markton is a half-day more at least from here and we don't have that kind of time. He's dying!" The Flea dropped to his knees and slapped his palms together as he looked to the heavens. "Oldam, please show mercy and help us." The big kid moaned in the dirt. The Flea squawked and prayed louder. "Oh, merciful Oldam, send us a miracle."

When Mags didn't budge, the brush to the side of the road rustled and a grim young woman with a crossbow stepped out onto the road. The girl was slight, like the Flea, and from their shared dirty blonde hair and freckled faces, Mags took them for siblings. In temperament, however, they were quite different. The girl stayed calm and her hands only shook a little as she aimed the crossbow at Mags. Her face was hard, but her eyes twitched a little, nervous ticks. Still she stayed calm and believed herself to be in charge.

"Get off that horse," the girl ordered.

"A crossbow is a bad choice. Reloading is slow and difficult," Mags said.

"That won't matter if I hit you the first time," the girl said.

"You're sure you can?" Mags asked.

The girl narrowed her eyes. "Do you really want to find out?"

Mags smiled and held up her hands. "Okay then." She dismounted and stood beside Duck.

Bog struggled and held up his hands. "Hey! Untie me and I'll help you."

The big kid opened his eyes and got to his feet. He didn't make eye contact with Mags, and she noted that. He bit his lip and looked embarrassed and ashamed. They weren't professionals.

The girl with the crossbow narrowed her eyes and looked at Bog for a moment. "Why are you tied up?"

"She kidnapped me," Bog replied. He held up his hands again. "Hey, I know where there's a good score. I'll take you to it. I swear."

"Shut up. We'll decide what's what." The girl nodded her head toward the big kid. "Get him off that horse, but don't untie him."

"Good call," Mags said.

The girl scowled at her and gripped the crossbow tighter. "You shut up too."

"Ava, he says he'll put us onto a big score." The Flea hopped around and fidgeted. He pointed to Bog. "We should untie him."

"What's the score?" Ava asked.

"I know where there's a payroll. Where are we? Rousland? Easy to steal. I'll take you right to it." Bog held up his hands. "Come on. I don't have any weapons."

"She tied him up for a reason." The big kid's voice rumbled deep.

"I'm not stupid, Dane," Ava said. "We'll take you with us, and you'll show us the job." She pointed the crossbow briefly at Bog. "Dane, Eldon, grab the horses."

Mags whistled and both Duck and Goose reared, then they took off down the road. Bog fell into the dirt and the two boys squawked and dove out of the way. The commotion frightened Ava, and she jerked the crossbow back toward Mags. In the same motion, she pulled at the trigger. The bolt lodged in Mag's stomach. Mags grimaced and fell to her knees.

Ava dropped the crossbow and a look of fear and panic crossed her face. Dane got to his feet and scrambled over to Mags.

"Ava! What did you do?" He looked toward Mag's stomach and then to his companion. "We have to help her."

"I-I didn't mean to!" Ava yelled. She took a step toward Mags as if she wanted to help, but then another emotion flashed across the girl's face and she hardened her features.

"There's only one way to deal with her," Bog said.

They all looked to Bog, who had managed to pick up the crossbow.

"Bog, you're going to regret . . ." Mags started, but she didn't finish the sentence. Bog hit her in the head with the crossbow and everything went black.

CHAPTER
SIX

When Mags opened her eyes, Duck and Goose had returned and were grazing at the side of the road. The group of idiots was gone. Her head throbbed. She reached up and touched the place and found a large knot where Bog had struck her. When she moved her arm, a blinding hot flash of pain rippled through her stomach, which made her forget about the knot on her head. She looked down at her abdomen. The crossbow bolt stuck in her right side. It had penetrated nearly to the fletching, which stuck out about two inches from the wound. She winced as she reached around her side and looked for the exit. The bolt hadn't exited, but she felt the place where the arrowhead had nearly burst through the skin. Close to her right kidney.

"Great. Just great," Mags said. Her muscles and guts screamed at her as she got to her knees. A wave of pain hit her again and she collapsed back into the dirt. Mags lay there in the road and closed her eyes as she tried to steady herself enough to stand.

The girl hadn't meant to shoot her. Her face had a look of horror on it when she realized what she'd done. That told Mags the trio hadn't really been planning on hurting anyone. Most likely, none of them had ever killed anyone before. The fact they left her for dead didn't read so much as cold to her as shocked. The big kid, Dane, had wanted to help; it was his first instinct. The skinny kid—Eldon apparently, but the Flea fit him much better—had panicked and the girl, Ava, was pretending to be a hard case. That was much more dangerous than an actual hard case.

The pain began to mix with anger and annoyance as she lay there. She had known the kids were planning something and she had been over-confident that their plan was idiotic and that she'd be able to handle it. In hindsight, Mags thought she should have gotten ahead of them and taught them how a proper ambush worked. But then she winced as she realized they had done just fine ambushing her even if they hadn't meant to kill her. That grudging bit of self-reflection annoyed her again and the anger at her situation and at losing Bog a second time made her hand burn and the red scar on her cheek sizzle.

"No!"

This time the voice was emphatic and clearly a woman.

"Who is that? What do you mean, no?" Mags yelled.

"No!"

The voice didn't answer with any new information. It just repeated the word.

Mags screamed in frustration but the effort invited the pain to jolt through her again. She took a deep breath then exhaled and calmed. She controlled it and slowly sat up. She would deal with the trio and Bog. But first, she had to deal with the crossbow bolt.

She couldn't just yank it out. Well, she could, but that was the hard way. The head was close to exiting. She'd just have to help it a bit. Mags looked around and found a suitable tree just off the road. It was wide and easy to get to. She grimaced and bit her lip against the pain but was finally able to stand. She shuffled over to the tree. The horses followed and nickered their moral support.

Mags grasped the fletching in her left hand and snapped it off. Waves of pain and nausea coursed through her. She fell to her knees and waited for it to dull. When it was manageable again, she stood up, took a deep breath and shoved herself against the tree trunk.

"Bukker's Seventh Cock!" Mags clung to the tree and panted as the pain screamed through her side. When she calmed, she reached back and felt for the arrowhead. It now stuck out through her back. She grabbed it and pulled. After what seemed an eternity of long, slow pulling and loud screaming, Mags finally yanked it free. She collapsed against the tree, still grasping the crossbow bolt. Duck and Goose whinnied at her and nudged her with their noses.

"I'm alright." She patted them, then used their necks to pull herself up. Blood burbled from both the entrance and the exit, staining her shirt. She pulled a couple of rags from her saddlebag and wiped up the worst of it, but the wounds stopped bleeding without much attention on her part. The flesh grew hot and tingled. Mags felt her heartbeat increase and the half that belonged to the hound seemed to beat a bit faster. As it did, the wounds began to close. It was tender and still agony to move much, but it was manageable. She took a drink from her water skin and washed the blood off herself, then she put the crossbow bolt in her bag.

"I think I'm going to put that back where it came from," she said, envisioning jamming it somewhere non-lethal.

The horses stamped their feet and whinnied. Mags leaned against them and put her head against Duck's neck. The pleasant smell of the horse and his big, steady heartbeat calmed her and helped her block out the discomfort as her wound healed. After about a half hour, the hole was closed and while still sore, no longer an impediment to her movement. She patted Duck in thanks for his support. The big black horse bumped her gently with his head.

"Alright. Let's see if we can find these stupid kids." Mags looked around for tracks and easily found where the party of idiots had run off into the forest. They had been dumb enough to follow a path. If they were going to do that they should have just made it easier and stuck to the road. Mags sighed. She had a feeling nothing the trio did would ever be the easy thing.

CHAPTER

SEVEN

A fter about an hour of tracking, she heard them ahead. Mags signaled to the horses and they stopped. She dropped their reins near a small tree. "If this goes south, you two beat it."

The horses shook their heads at her, as if nodding in the affirmative, but silently. They were uncommonly intelligent horses.

Mags patted them both, then snuck off into the underbrush until she got close enough to observe the camp.

"We shouldn't have left her!" The big kid protested, sounding sad and ashamed. His voice cracked and he was emotional.

"Don't cry for that bitch, sonny," Bog said. "We should have chopped off her head. That's the only way to be rid of her. Now she'll find us for sure."

"No way. Ava skewered her good." The Flea's voice shook when he spoke. He didn't sound impressed, but more surprised and incredulous that Bog could think Mags was anything but dead.

"Kid, you don't know bounty hunters, do you? They don't

stop. And you especially don't know that bounty hunter. If you did, you'd know we need to get going and pick up the pace or she's gonna get us by dark."

"There's no way she can follow the trail in the condition she was in," Ava said.

Mags smiled as the girl's voice cracked and then toughened, as if she were forcing herself to keep up the pretense of not caring.

"That bounty hunter can follow any trail in any condition. You have no idea who she is, do you?" Bog asked.

"No, should I?" the girl said, cocky amusement in her voice.

"Yes. But since you didn't let me take her head, you're gonna find out who she is."

Mags unsheathed both her batons and was about to validate everything Bog had just said, but stopped when she heard a loud snap and something big move on the other side of the camp. The group of idiots heard it too and all heads turned toward the noise. Before any of them could be ready for a fight, five large hairy warriors stepped into the circle. They were Norrik raiders, covered in wolf fur and full to the brim with grim attitude. They trained crossbows on everyone and the biggest one stepped forward with his great sword drawn.

"You stupid little shits."

The Flea went to jump up, which made two of the bowman growl, and point their weapons at him. The big kid pulled him back down, and they all held up their hands. Still, the Flea didn't have sense enough to keep quiet.

"Look, Ulf . . . Hey . . . We were just . . . You know how it is, we were on our way to pay you back, but then we did a job in Havelock, and-and then we ran into this sure thing on the road, and now we're onto an even bigger score, so if you wait . . . Yeah we can—"

Ulf slapped the kid, an open-handed slap that knocked him

flat to the ground. "We know all about Havelock. What did Angmere tell you about pretending to be Anniks?"

"What do you care so long as we produce?" Ava scowled at him. Her hand twitched toward her own crossbow. Mags held her breath. If the girl touched that crossbow, the Norrik would slaughter the lot of morons.

"No!"

The voice boomed in her ears this time, making her skull feel like it was vibrating. The girl's hand stayed still and the voice quieted. Mags calmed herself and stayed hidden. She wasn't afraid of the Norrikmen but she did respect their reputations as warriors and she was heavily outnumbered. She wanted Bog back but anything she did here wouldn't result in that.

"For seven hundred years, Anniks have raided and done as we liked. We don't take Rousland brats to breast." Ulf held his sword to Ava's throat. She glared at him and set her jaw, defiant even in a position of no power. "Besides, where's the production? We've seen no coin, no plunder."

Ava flinched and for just a second, Mags saw fear flash across her face, just as it had when the girl had shot her. But just like then, it was brief, and the girl glowered and stuck out her lip in a huffing pout.

"That's what I thought," Ulf said. "I wanted to track you down and skin you alive, but Angmere commanded I bring you back. Selfish bastard wants the pleasure for himself. But what are you gonna do? He's the boss."

Bog chose that moment to speak. He stood up slowly with his palms open. "I got nothing to do with them. I'll just be on my way."

Ulf laughed. "It surely looks like you've something to do with them. Nobody would have these idiots around unless they had a good reason."

"Ulf, look, see he's got a line on a huge score. Easy money.

We'll split it with you." The Flea recovered himself enough to try his slick-talk again.

"Well, that's honorable of you. I'm sure Angmere will be touched by it when you try that line out on him in person. Of course, I doubt you'll have a tongue after, but he'll probably appreciate the gesture." Ulf nodded at his companions and they motioned with the crossbows for everyone to get up. "Let's go. He's waiting."

"It's the middle of the night," Ava scoffed.

"It's barely a half-hour past sundown and there's a big moon. The sooner we get back to Annik, the sooner the fun starts." He pushed the tip of his blade into Ava's neck.

"NO!"

The woman's voice screamed and Mags held her ears.

Ava winced at the prick of the blade but didn't cry out. Ulf lowered his blade, then motioned with it. "Get up and get moving or I'll stick you right here. Angmere'll get over it."

"Ava." It was the first time the big kid spoke. It wasn't lost on Mags he was the only one who kept quiet and did the smart thing.

Ava looked over at him and her face softened a second. She looked up at Ulf, still defiant. "Fine."

He didn't allow them to gather their gear but herded them all in between the bowmen. The group started off into the brush.

Mags stayed put. She waited until they were far enough away, then she crept into the circle and put out the fire. A quick rummage through their bags yielded nothing of value. She thought for a moment. Dealing with Norrikmen was only slightly better than dealing with the Tyrraneans. Mags hated the violent, posturing nonsense that was always on full display from them. That was annoying but could be handled. What was more difficult was dealing with their wasteful cruelty. This Ulf fellow was a prime example. Mags had traveled extensively through

Norrik and she knew that all of his talk of flaying and skewering wasn't just for show. He meant it. She'd seen awful things done by Norrik raiders and she knew he wasn't making idle threats. The trio was in trouble. What Mags had to consider was if she had a way to save them. Immortal she might be, but it would still be extremely difficult if not impossible for her to fight her way through an entire clan of Norrikmen. Her earlier issues had tempered her confidence.

The second thing to consider was if Bog was really worth it. Mags took a certain amount of pride in her work. If she took a job, she saw it done. That wasn't to say she hadn't lost bounties before, but that was mostly to other hunters who had found the mark before she did. Mags generally didn't lose a mark once she'd found them, and the fact that she'd now lost Bog twice stuck in her craw. Still, that was pride and while pride could be a good thing—something that helped you work hard and stay focused—when it was a spiteful thing it usually just messed things up.

Mags could afford to let Bog go. She wasn't flush with coin, but jobs were plentiful. She didn't need to get Bog back, and she certainly didn't need to worry about a trio of kids who seemed proficient at getting themselves in trouble. The smart play was to turn around and head back down the Trades toward Greenshade where work was in abundance.

"No! Find them!"

The voice was adamant.

"Alright, I've had enough of this shi—wow!" Mags held her ears as the voice screamed.

"No! Find them! No! Find them! No! Find them!"

"Alright! Just shut up! I'll find them!" Mags screamed back. She looked around to the sky. Was it a god messing with her? This wasn't the style of any of the gods she knew, this cryptic whispering and screaming, but she was far to the North and didn't have much interaction with these deities. When nobody materialized or screamed at her further, Mags assumed they were appeased with her acquiescence. She started back the way she'd come and collected the horses. She didn't bother to track the party through the forest; she knew where Annik was. The only concern she had was arriving there in time to save the idiots' lives. She mounted Duck and took off at a steady canter down the road. Goose followed.

Ulf was right. The moon was full and bright. It was an excellent night to travel.

EIGHT

Mags made good time and as she was mounted, was able to catch up to the party quickly. That didn't matter. They were going to Annik, a backwater clan enclave on the southern shore of the Raider's Sea. The proximity to Tyrrane made her itch.

Even though she caught up, she kept her distance. She briefly contemplated sneaking in the dark and taking Bog's head, salvage at least half her money, but every time she even considered changing her plan, the voice screamed at her and the longer she followed, the louder and more painful it was in her head. She didn't know who or what the voice was but she knew she had to save them.

Even still, the idiots were in trouble. Mags didn't know Ulf and had never even heard of any chieftain named Angmere, but in no place in the world did owing money ever lead to anything good—and dodging only delayed the violence. She needed to get the trio and Bog out of there. She hoped this war chieftain, Angmere, could be reasoned with, bargained with, and she could resolve the issue. She sighed. "Well, at least I'm not in Tyrrane."

Two warriors guarded the entrance to the walled village, although calling it a wall was generous. Barely taller than an average-sized man, they had slapped it together with saplings and mud, new in some places, worn and rickety in others, with no watch towers or ramparts. Their only attempt at defense was a few clusters of pikes shoved in the ground, but they were sparse and so far apart that Duck and Goose could stand side-by-side between them. They were no deterrent at all. However, they had bothered to paint threatening war symbols in red all over. The whole place wouldn't withstand an attack from a litter of kittens, let alone a respectable raiding party. All in all, it gave the impression of a play fort constructed by children with materials from a junk pile. Even so, Mags couldn't dismiss them, but now she felt her chances of resolving her issues with Bog and the trio were even worse.

Mags nodded at the guards. "I'm here to see your chieftain, Angmere."

"Why?" the guard on the left asked.

"I come with a business proposition," Mags said.

The guards looked at one another and sniggered. "Business eh? We can give you business."

Bile rose in her throat, and Mags clenched her left hand in a fist. The bones ached and the muscles twitched as she envisioned the cobalt blade taking their heads in two strokes so swift they wouldn't see them coming, but the blade wasn't hers to command. Instead, she took a deep breath, tamped down her disgust, then gave them a smile and a wink. "I'm sure you can, but it's likely in our mutual best interest if I see him first. We don't make the rules, huh?" She shrugged.

As they eyed her, Mags concluded they were doing their best to determine her threat level. It was almost painful to watch their brains work. Her weapons weren't big and impressive and in their eyes she was only a woman and not particularly dangerous. It often worked to her advantage in this part of the world.

Finally, they nodded at her. Duck walked through the gate as soon as it entered Mag's mind.

The muddy path led up a slight mound to a hall. It looked a bit better constructed than the fortifications, but not by much. The same red war runes decorated it, as well as some skulls on pikes. The skulls were bleached white from the wind and sun. Old and small, Mags theorized they came from an old barrow rather than an execution.

She dismounted and patted Duck and Goose. "Stay sharp, fellas."

The horses nickered at her and stomped their feet. They both turned around and faced the gate. Mags smiled. "Good idea." She patted them one last time before she entered the hall.

The inside of the Chieftain's Hall did not match the rest of the shoddy compound. Ornate torches lit the large room in a soft, yellow glow. The tables were heavy oak, well-used, and intact, without the normal knife marks she had seen in most taverns and halls where the Norrikmen gathered. Statues, idols, and tapestries decorated the room and Mags nearly laughed aloud. All of it was looted from some place south. Nothing in the tapestries or in the art looked native to Norrik.

What Mags assumed was the great chieftain Angmere held court from a dais in the back of the hall. He sat on a throne with plush furs, well-attended by serving girls and surrounded by his captains. The big one Ulf sat to his right. To his left stood a tall, thin woman with white-blonde hair dressed in a black drape dress. The woman tilted her head when she saw Mags, as if she recognized her. Mags had no idea who the woman was but when the woman looked to Mags's left hand and smiled, she knew she'd been made. It wasn't uncommon, but it surprised her this far north. Perhaps the woman wasn't from the North. Something about the look in her eyes worried Mags, sending off the warning bells in her head and giving her an uncomfortable, nasty feeling in her guts. Bargaining for the trio was going to be difficult.

The trio and Bog hung by their feet suspended from the rafters. They were all bound and gagged and looked a little beat up, but they were alive. Bog and the Flea squirmed when they saw her. The other two stayed still. She ignored them and turned her attention to the chieftain.

Angmere's dress was opulent for a war chieftain. His furs were ornate and he wore a lot of jewelry to the point of ridiculousness. Rings adorned all of his fingers and Mags reckoned he had at least ten pounds of gold chain around his neck. It didn't say fearsome warrior to her, but the years had taught Mags many lessons and first among them was looks could be deceiving.

Mags bowed from the neck and waited to be addressed.

Angmere gulped down some wine, then wiped his mouth and beard with the back of his hand. He belched, a long, loud noise, then he looked Mags up and down. "Who are you?"

"Magdalena Verran." Mags bowed again. "Thank you for receiving me in your beautiful hall."

"Receiving you?" Angmere laughed and looked at his fellows. "I like that. Very official. Kingly." He puffed up, lifted his cup in Mag's direction. "What do you want?"

"She wants her bounty," the tall blonde woman said. Her voice had a deep, rusty quality. It was an old-sounding voice for someone who looked so young.

"A bounty hunter?" Angmere toasted her again. "I always wanted to be a bounty hunter, but you only get half for heads and cutting the heads off is the part I like best. Too bad it's not good business." He held his cup up and a girl refilled it. "Why would your bounty be here?"

"Well, I'd say he was in the wrong place at the wrong time." Mags nodded to the idiots suspended from the rafters. "He was with those three when your man found them."

41

Bog yelled something unintelligible into his gag and wriggled. Mags pointed to him. "He's wanted in Deep Knotting."

"Oh yeah? Is he worth a lot?" Angmere asked.

And there it was, the question Mags had been hoping Angmere wasn't smart enough to ask.

"He won't make anyone rich, but I take whatever work comes these days."

"Can't be picky, I guess. So what was he doing with those three?" Angmere belched again and waved his cup toward the trio.

"They claimed to be working with him on some big job," Ulf said. "He was tied up when we found them. They said they took him from someone on the road."

Angmere chortled. "You must be a terrible bounty hunter if those three got the drop on you. But I suppose you're only a woman." He looked to Ulf, who also laughed and nodded in agreement.

"May none here ever find out how clever a hunter she really is," the blonde said. She put a hand on Angmere's shoulder and leaned close. "My lord, she's Matchi's Hound."

"You're not from the North," Mags said, regarding the woman. The icky feeling she had when she first saw the woman returned and increased.

"I am from everywhere," the woman said.

"My sorceress, Geta," Angmere said. He puffed up again, full of swaggering boast. "Name me another clan that has a sorceress."

"An impressive addition to your court," Mags said. She had a clear measure of the situation now. The woman was no sorceress. She might be a magic user, but this was no great seat of power and never had been. Angmere was new to his wealth and quite obviously an idiot. But he was an idiot with an army and a magic user.

Angmere scoffed. "Now what was that you said this bounty

hunter lady is? Matchi's Hound? That's just an old story to frighten Darrish brats. Oldam would never allow it."

"If Darrish lost the bounty to them, and we took the bounty, seems like he's ours," Ulf said.

"Exactly." Angmere clanked his cup to Ulf's.

"But then you'd have to go all the way to Deep Knotting to collect. He's of little value to a great chieftain, such as you."

"Maybe not, but he'll be good sport, just like those three will be." Angmere motioned toward the trio. "Ulf, did anyone catch a bear yet? I can't decide if I want to feed them to a bear or if I want to skin them alive."

"No bears yet," Ulf said.

"Disappointing," Mags said. The conversation was not going as she'd hoped. Angmere was too much of an idiot.

Mags caught the girl, Ava, looking at her. The girl didn't struggle. She hung calmly while her companions fidgeted. She stared at Mags, not asking for help, but almost like she was telling Mags off, acting as though she didn't need help. Mags knew better.

"My Lord, don't we have need of a bounty hunter? Perhaps a bargain may be struck?" Geta said, smiling as she stroked Angmere's shoulder. "Perhaps we should invite her to stay and make her welcome while we discuss."

"We don't need a bounty hunter. I can handle—" Ulf's temper flared but Geta cut him off.

"We should retire and counsel," Geta said. "My Lord?"

Angmere looked up at the woman and nodded. "Yes. I'll take some rest before supper. Come to my quarters, both of you."

When Angmere stood up, everyone else in the hall did as well and waited. He pointed at Mags. "We'll decide at Feast. You stay here."

"Don't try anything, Darrish," Ulf said, sneering at Mags. "Or do. I like a meal after a fight."

Mags ignored him and addressed Angmere. "I'm honored by your hospitality." She bowed her head again.

"Good. Very good. Nice manners on that one, for a bounty hunter," Angmere said. He tottered a bit when he went to step down from the dais. Geta and Ulf steadied him and led him out. Everyone else filed out after them, leaving Mags alone with the prisoners. She walked over and smiled at them.

"Hello, idiots."

CHAPTER
NINE

The Flea and Bog screamed into their gags and flailed, which only caused them to swing. The big kid did nothing, but his eyes were wide as he looked at Mags. The girl simply stared.

Mag grabbed Bog and stopped his swinging. "Your bounty is not worth all this hassle." She punched him in the face and he went slack and silent. "As for you three—"

The Flea struggled and his lips moved double time against his gag. Mags rolled her eyes and slipped his gag out of his mouth.

"Thank Oldam, you're alive! Hey, that business on the road was all just a big misunderstanding. Look, get us out of here and we'll help you do whatever needs doing."

"Oh, did I misunderstand you shooting me and leaving me to die?"

"That-that-that was an accident. Junk trigger. Ava got nervy."

Ava glared at him. The big kid spoke into his gag to the Flea.

"No, I won't shut up, Dane. She's fine." He looked at Mags and smiled. "All fine. Right as rain. Hey. We can help you, seriously."

"Doubtful," Mags said. She put the gag back in the Flea's mouth. He struggled and kept talking. "Shut up or be shut up." She motioned to Bog.

The Flea quieted.

Mags looked to Ava and stared at her a moment, then ungagged her.

"You should be dead," Ava said with no emotion in her voice.

"Many, many times over," Mags agreed.

"You should have just left us. You could have," Ava said.

"Yeah, well"—Mags struggled to explain. A disembodied voice commanding, no, annoying her to do things was odd, even for her—"I didn't. And, unfortunately, we're now in a bind. If you want to live through this, keep your mouths shut."

"And I suppose you're going to get us out of this jam?" Ava asked.

"I'm going to get me out of this jam. You idiots are a big, fat maybe." She looked to the big kid, Dane. He looked like he wanted to say something. "What do you have to say?" She pulled his gag out.

"I'm sorry. We should have helped you." His deep voice rumbled and his eyes were kind and sincere.

Mags wanted to retort with something smart-ass about not needing the help of the stupid, but the kid really meant the apology. These were not bad kids. They seemed lost and as if they were playing at a game they had no experience or skill at, because they didn't have any other options. Only this game was going to get them killed. The thought of it darkened her heart and just seemed a waste to her. It wasn't like she hadn't seen waste before but here, so close to the end of her contract with Matchi and Kohoc, it hit her hard. They should have long lives ahead of them. But currently, they didn't.

"Help them. Please."

Mags took a deep breath and nodded, both to Dane and the voice.

"Live and learn. Maybe you learned and if you be quiet and stay ready, you may yet live," she said.

"I really don't see how," Ava said.

Mags replaced their gags and sat down on a bench to think. "Right now, neither do I, but hopefully it comes to me."

CHAPTER
TEN

After a few hours, Angmere and his court returned. He looked sleepy and was obviously still drunk, but he perked up when the meal was served. He and his lieutenants gorged themselves on meat: roast mutton, chicken, and ham. The serving girl plopped a bowl of gray fish stew down in front of Mags. At least she thought it was fish stew. It smelled fishy and the lumps in it resembled fish, but its consistency—that of regurgitated porridge—confused the pallet and turned the stomach. Apparently in his quest to become the premiere war chief of Norrik, Angmere hadn't mastered culinary skills nor hospitality quite yet.

His lack of courtly refinement and knowledge didn't faze him. He laughed and slurped ale as he chatted with Ulf and gnawed the meat from a bone. Ulf eyed Mags with a look of disgust. He would be trouble in this enterprise, that she knew. Whether because she was Darrish or a woman, she didn't know —likely both—but it was clear from the way he stared at her that he despised her. Mags didn't look away from his gaze. She politely stirred her fish porridge and glared back. Even when Ulf backhanded a servant for delaying filling his mug, Mags didn't flinch. She boiled inward, but any move on her part other than courtesy was likely to touch off the powder keg.

Geta also kept her gaze firmly fixed on Mags, but it was greed, not hate that reflected in her eyes. She sipped from a black obsidian wine goblet and smiled at her, the kind of smile that was half-way between covetous and predatory. After a bit, Geta took a pitcher of ale from one of the serving girls and refilled Angmere's mug herself. She leaned close to his ear but didn't whisper. "My lord, our guest awaits your decision."

Angmere took a drink of his ale and nodded. "Yes. Well, Bounty Hunter, I have a bounty for you. It's an easy one, two women. They stole from me and I want them back here for correction." He laughed and spilled ale down his face as he elbowed Ulf. "One of them is a great big bitch. Ugly. Blonde. Hard to miss. The other, well, she's the woman with the big ugly one. Nothing special." Angmere spat the words "nothing special" as if he were trying to convince people of it. From his tone and the look in his eye, the unremarkable blonde woman was in fact, quite special—and he hated her for it. "I'll give you oh . . . fifty copper for the pair. That's a windfall for you. I doubt a woman bounty hunter ever gets such a good job." He laughed and elbowed Ulf again, who chortled in agreement.

Mags felt the red place on her cheek burn and a great deal of creative curse words burble to her lips, however, she held them back and her temper in check. She managed a flat smile for them. "Thank you for your offer, but I'm afraid I'm already contracted."

Angmere ignored her refusal, which she assumed was the norm for him. He went on with details. "She went south, we think. What did you see, Geta? Kos?"

"Yes, my lord. I believe the traitors are heading to Kos." Geta smiled at Mags. "This is a wonderful opportunity for you."

"I'm sure it is and I'm honored to be considered, but I really have to say no. As I said, I'm already contracted and once I accept a contract, I am obligated to see it fulfilled. I could deliver my bounty in Deep Knotting and then head to Kos for you. It's close. I'm sure I could find— "

Geta held up a hand and interrupted. "I'm afraid that's not possible. My lord requires this done immediately. He needs the traitors returned by the Annik gathering on Midsummer."

"I can't deliver my charge to Deep Knotting, find your women, then return by then. It's quite impossible." Mags shook her head and did her best to keep her tone contrite and not dismissive. "I'm really very sorry that I can't help you."

"You're Matchi's Hound. For you, nothing is impossible," Geta said. The way she said it, silky and sensual, gave Mags the creeps and in no uncertain terms meant trouble.

"It's not quite that simple." Mags shook her head. A bad feeling started down in the pit of her stomach. The sorceress, or whatever she was, knew way too much. Something wasn't right. And Mags was sure of something else, if Angmere and this witch wanted the women for a clan moot, things were not going to go well for them.

"Really. I'm sorry, but I'm bound by code to deliver the bounty I was contracted for first before taking another. It's really just that simple."

Geta nodded. The predatory smile didn't dissipate from her face. She stroked Angmere's shoulders, then patted him before she stepped away. "As you please, my lord."

Angmere smiled a cruel smile, like a child given leave to stomp on ants. He looked at Ulf and nodded. They both laughed, then Ulf rose from the table and walked over to Bog. He turned and grinned at Mags, then unsheathed his over-large sword. With one swipe of the sword, Bog's head separated from his body. It hit the floor with a juicy thud. Blood spurted from Bog's neck and splattered beneath him as he swung from the rafter. The trio all recoiled and swung as they tried to avoid the gore. The smell of hot blood filled the air and all the Norrikmen in the hall laughed and cheered. They chanted Ulf's name.

Ulf picked up the severed head. He held it out toward Mags and laughed, a deep and hearty guffaw at the anger on her face. He threw Bog's head into the great firepit, then wiped his sword on Bog's clothing and sheathed the weapon before he sat back down at Angmere's side and resumed drinking.

Angmere chugged his ale, gave a loud belch, and held his cup out for more. He smiled at Geta, then at Mags. "That problem is solved."

Mags boiled with rage. Her left hand burned and ached, but the blade didn't form. If it did, she could slaughter the entire room before any of them could pull a sword and as she watched Bog's head burn and Angmere and Ulf laughing at her rage, she thought she could put aside any hesitation or guilt at taking lives. She could end them all and not blink.

But if she were honest with herself, even in her anger she couldn't just mow them all down. Angmere and Ulf she might not regret, at least not right away, but she'd have to kill everyone in the enclave and that wasn't something she was willing to do. Violence wasn't the answer. At least not yet.

All of the Norrik warriors laughed. Angmere raised a toast to his own cleverness and Ulf focused on Mags and smiled. His hand twitched on the pommel of his sword as he silently dared Mags to pull a weapon.

Geta studied her as well. The woman cocked her head and the look on her face was a mixture of amusement and curiosity. For some reason, Mags found her the most infuriating one of all and as she looked at her, her left hand tingled ever so slightly and the muscles in it twitched. Mags looked down at her limb that had darkened to the blue of the deep sea, like it was going to turn, but it didn't. It just twitched and ached. Mags flexed it a few times, calmed herself, and exhaled slowly before speaking.

"Indeed. Well, that contract is void now. However, I still respectfully decline."

"Decline?" Angmere stopped laughing and threw his mug against the wall. He stamped his feet like an angry toddler as he looked to Geta, then to Ulf. "She can't do that! You said she wouldn't do that!"

"We don't need her. I'll go get those whores and I'll end this Darrish one now." Ulf pulled his sword and advanced.

"No! Wait! Ulf!" Geta's gravel voice boomed in the hall, shaking the rafters. Everyone stopped.

Mag's right hand was on her baton. Her left-hand glowed blue.

"There's a better way," Geta said. The woman closed her eyes and mumbled something in a different language. From the look on their faces nobody else in the room understood it. Nobody except Mags.

"Son of a Bitch." Mags felt a familiar burn in her stomach and her head throbbed as her vision went red. She dropped to one knee and clenched her teeth as she bowed her head and avoided being blinded by the bright blue flash of light.

CHAPTER

ELEVEN

his had better be good!" Matchi yelled.

The Huntress's voice reverberated and shook the walls of the hall. Everyone in the hall froze in place. Their faces were locked in grimaces, blinded by the bright light. They were momentarily in stasis, stuck there until Matchi decided they weren't. Everyone except Mags and Geta. Geta looked pleased with herself. She clasped her hands in glee and smiled broadly. Mags sighed.

When Matchi saw Mags, she rolled her eyes. "You. Why is it always you? Did you summon me? You know I hate that."

"Of course not," Mags said. She had long since given up being humbly differential to the great goddess. Now she could barely be minimally respectful. In fact, she really couldn't be described as even minimally respectful, only just submissive enough to Matchi to avoid Torment. And even in that she often failed. Still, she remained kneeling, forced into reverence, and that burned her even more.

"I summoned you, Great Goddess." Geta bowed. "We have need of your hound."

"Do I look like a merchant to you? My hound isn't for hire.

And anyway, she's got too many jobs as it is." Matchi looked around the room and squinted her eyes. "Where am I?"

"Norrik," Mags said.

"Ugh. Really? No wonder it smells of dead fish. Trust you, Magdalena, to be in this backward octopus's crotch." Matchi wrinkled her nose.

"Great Goddess. Loan us your hound. Something of great value was stolen from us and only she can recover it." Geta approached and knelt.

"Oh, I very much doubt that. You don't need my hound. Whatever it is probably reeks of dead fish. Just follow the stench. Besides, what could you people possibly have of great value?" Matchi scanned the hall with a look of disdain on her face.

"It's of value to us. So much so that we can promise something you greatly desire in return." Geta bowed lower.

Matchi laughed. "This should be good. What?"

Geta raised her head and smiled at her—a cocky, knowing smile. "We know where to find the Black Archer."

Mags shook her head. "Impossible. Nobody knows that."

"Shut up, Magdalena." Matchi held up a hand and Mags burned with pain. She looked to Geta, whose smile faded when she saw the rage radiate from the goddess. Matchi's voice was deadly serious. "Impossible. Nobody knows that."

"We do. And we will tell you. If you employ your hound and find it for us."

Matchi grabbed the woman and yanked her to her feet. "Don't toy with me." Her eyes glowed blue and lightning crackled through the rafters.

"We would never," Geta said. She held her palms up. "When she delivers our bounty before the Midsummer gathering, we will give you what you desire."

"And what's to stop me from torturing you into telling me what you know right now?" Matchi asked.

"The world knows the Great Huntress to be honorable. A fair proposal has been offered and isn't it a small thing for one so great and powerful as the Huntress?"

Mag's snorted and laughed. "Honorable?"

"Shut up, Magdalena! Torment!" Matchi's voice boomed and Mags covered her ears. A tall, impossibly skinny young man with greasy jet-black hair and wide, black eyes materialized beside Matchi.

"Oh, shit," Mags said.

Matchi nodded at her. "Oh yes. Torment. Demonstrate."

"Gladly! Hello, Magdalena. It's always so good to see you."

"You can go piss up a rope—" Mag's retort was cut short when Torment unleashed a violent stream of energy at her. As it ripped through her body, Mags screamed and twisted in agony. The voices all came rushing at her, screaming in her ears and filling her head with memories of heads and death.

"Alright. I think she gets it," Matchi said.

"But I only got started and she's always so tasty," Torment pouted. He kept on with the pain.

"Torment!" Matchi yelled. She threw up her hands in frustration. "What does it take to get decent minions?"

"As you wish, sister." Torment sighed as he raised his hands and stopped the flow of energy.

He bent down and smiled at Mags. She winced, not from the pain but from the foul odor of burnt hair and rot that emanated from him. He ignored her and leaned closer as she gagged.

"Only a mouthful this time, but of course, if ever you need my help, all I ask for is an entree." He kissed her on the cheek and laughed as she recoiled. "Toodles," Torment waved as he disappeared in a cloud of green vapor.

"You are powerful and honorable, Great Huntress. Nobody questions it. Show your honor and beneficence. Lend us your hound. You have nothing to lose and everything to gain."

Matchi stared at Geta a moment. She then threw the woman to the ground. "All right."

"Are you kidding me?" Mags yelled.

Matchi held up a hand and the pain forced Mags to the ground. "Shut up, Magdalena." She turned back to Geta. "I am honorable, but beneficence has never been my strong suit. If I do this and you do not give me what I want, you will understand much more about me than you bargained for. Magdalena, arm."

Mags had no choice. Matchi would have her way. But even still, the now familiar voice boomed in Mag's ears. *"No!"*

Mags winced. It was loud and she still had a headache from Torment, but she had an idea. "Fine. But I need something." She pointed to the Trio. "Those three. They owe me and I want them. Give them to me and I'll see it done."

"Magdalena, you'll see it done anyway. Now hold out your arm."

Mags closed her eyes and focused. "Kohoc."

Kohoc the Harvester appeared in a puff of black smoke. He pulled back his hood to reveal his gaunt, serious face, then wrinkled his nose. "It stinks of fish here. Is this Norrik?"

"Yes. Look, I need those three over there. Grant me them and I'll give you three more souls." Mag's stomach churned at the thought but she could see no other way.

"Mags, you can't mean that." Kohoc approached her and put a hand on her shoulder. His voice was gentle. "You're almost done."

"I know. I'm at 999. What's three more now?"

"Pain. And many lifetimes, possibly," Kohoc said.

"I know what I'm doing. Please." Mags looked up at him and gave him a genuine smile. "It's the right thing to do. I feel it."

Kohoc's face remained serious. "Then it shall be done." He looked to Matchi. "She adds three, sister. That's my price."

"You're getting soft in your old age," Matchi said. "Fine. Magdalena finds whatever this thing of great value is, by

56

Midsummer, and you give me what I want. She gets those three." Matchi's eyes narrowed and she gave Mags her slickest smile, the one that Mags had learned to dread as it always meant trouble. "Magdalena, should you fail me in this task, those three"—Matchi inclined her head towards the hanging Trio—"die. And you will do it."

"No!" The voice screamed inside Mag's head and she held her hands to her ears until it stopped.

"Matchi, don't bring them into it. I'll find the bounty," Mags said.

"Oh, I know you will. And you'll do it by Midsummer so I get my information or you take their heads. Both of you, arms." She pointed at both Mags and Geta. They held out their arms and Matchi touched each just above the wrist.

The flesh burned bright blue. Mags gritted her teeth. It hurt, but it was nothing compared to what else Matchi could do. Geta screamed. Eventually the pain dulled to a throb and the blue spot disappeared. After she marked Mags and Geta, she walked over to the Trio. She put a finger on each of their foreheads and the print glowed blue for a second or two, then it disappeared.

"There. Marked." She regarded them for a moment. "Eh, nothing special about them. You do get yourself in the worst trouble, Magdalena, and never for any good reason. Oh well." Matchi sniffed her own clothes. "Disgusting. I'm going to smell like fish for days. Now, if that's all from you lot, I'll be going back to more civilized places, ones that don't smell like a mermaid's cu—" She disappeared with the same flash of blue light she'd arrived in.

Kohoc stepped to Mags and shook his head sadly. "I feel like this is a much worse bargain than you know." He put a thin, sallow hand on Mag's shoulder, then with the other, tipped her chin up to look at him. "You must be cautious."

Mags understood he wasn't talking about Matchi. Mags looked over his shoulder at Geta. Geta stayed well back from

Kohoc. Her face did not reflect cockiness, but fear. If she had known the real Kohoc, the kind version, as Mags did, she would feel something else. Mags looked up to him and smiled, grateful. "I will be. And thank you."

He gave her a hint of a smile, one that barely changed the slope of his thin lips, but still a smile. A monumental thing for him and not something many had ever seen. "You won't be. But please do try." He backed away from her and disappeared in a slowly forming cloud of black smoke, as was his way.

When all the gods were gone, everyone else in the room woke up. They pulled their hands away from their eyes, no longer blinded, but confused as to what had happened. They didn't seem to know any time had passed.

Angmere fell off his throne. He thrashed around, drunk, angry, and confused as his court tried to help him up. "What just happened? Don't touch me!" He looked to Mags and Geta. "Explain or I'll have everyone's head!"

It was even more difficult to take him seriously as he flailed like a turtle on its back, but Mags did her best. She gave him a little bow. "All right. I'll accept your bounty. I will find these women and return them by Midsummer. My price is those three." She pointed to the Trio.

Angmere's face blackened in anger. He looked to Geta. "What's this? I didn't agree to this!"

"It's all right, my lord. Remember what we gain." Geta waved her hand at him and looked at Ulf. Ulf's face was red and angry as well, but he calmed when Geta looked at him. Angmere did as well.

"Fine. Take them. You'd better deliver, bounty hunter, or I'll mount your head above my fire and make boots from their skin." Angmere settled back into his throne and accepted a mug of ale from Geta. He slurped it and glowered.

"You're a man not to be crossed. The bargain is struck. I'll deliver what was promised." Mags looked to Geta. "You'd be wise to do the same."

Ulf stomped and snorted like an angry bear. He pointed at Mags. "We can't trust a Darrish whore! She's a woman. She can't do this. She won't do this! Angmere, send me. I'll bring them back and they'll wish for—"

"The contract is done. Talk to your sorceress." Mags paused at the word for a beat and eyed Geta, so the woman would know the disregard Mags bore her.

Anger at the insult flared across Geta's face, but she only responded to Ulf. "You will have your day, my love. Patience." Geta soothed him with her hands, as she had done Angmere. Ulf growled but dropped his arm. "She'll fail. And when she does, I'll make her pay."

"Maybe and maybe not," Mags said. She saluted Ulf, then spat on the ground. She retrieved three knives from her belt and threw them at the ropes suspending Ava, Dane, and the Flea. The throwing knives sliced through the ropes cleanly, and the Trio hit the ground hard.

They boys groaned and rolled around. Ava made no noise. She got to her feet quickest and held out her hands. Mags cut the bonds. Ava shrugged off the ropes and helped Dane to his feet, who pulled the still complaining Flea up to his feet. Mags cut Dane's hands free, but left the Flea bound. It seemed like a good idea. She also left his gag in place. That seemed like an even better idea.

"Keep your mouths shut," she growled. "Move. Now."

They obeyed. The Trio hurried out of the hall, Dane and Ava pulling the Flea along. Mags didn't rush. She bowed to Angmere, then she eyeballed Ulf and smiled.

He unsheathed his sword and growled.

Geta put her hand on his arm. "Patience."

This time, he didn't sheath the weapon. "Patience."

"I wish you good fortune until we meet again." Mags bowed to them all and followed the Trio out of the hall.

Once outside, she whistled to Duck and Goose and led them all out of the Annik enclave as quickly as she could without looking like she was doing it as quickly as she could. The Trio followed her lead: Ava, then the Flea, and the big kid in the rear. When they got about a quarter mile away from the enclave, the Flea bounded up to Mags and somehow spat out his gag.

"Hey, great work. My name's Eldon, by the way. The big guy is Dane. The girl is my little sister, Ava. Mags, is it? Great. Hey, I don't know how you talked them into this, but I couldn't have done it better myself. Only maybe you could—"

The voice in Mag's head drowned him out even as Mags thought about punching him. *"No."*

It elongated the word this time. It wasn't so strong in the negative. Apparently it knew Mags could only take so much.

Mags stopped. The party all stopped. The big kid, Dane, looked apologetic. The girl, Ava, scowled. Mags stared at the Flea. "Put the gag back on."

"But we're clear and—"

Mags said nothing. She just stared at him and quirked an eyebrow.

Ava smacked Eldon on the back of the head. He rubbed his head and scowled at her.

Mags whistled to the horses and they resumed their walk.

Everyone had the intelligence—even the disembodied voice, at least for a little while—to shut up.

CHAPTER

TWELVE

Mags kept the party moving at a fast pace and didn't stop until the sun was quite low in the sky and she had no choice but to make camp. She was relieved to see the Trio needed no instruction as to what to do to set up a camp, at least Ava and Dane didn't. The big guy set about gathering firewood. Ava took the waterskins and filled them from the river. The Flea, Eldon, sat down on a log and rubbed at his wrists as he kicked up his feet and propped them up on the log.

"Well, that was a close shave, but hey, we always manage to get out of those, huh?" He grinned at Mags. "So, partner, what's our play?"

His voice irritated her and frayed her already spent nerves. She ignored him and went to work taking care of the horses. Mags unsaddled them and closed her eyes as she breathed in their comforting smell. She worked on Duck first, currying him, then brushing him until his black coat shone. But neither she nor the horses could relax as they normally would during the process. When she ignored him and moved away, Eldon hopped up and danced all around them, chattering and giving opinions.

Duck's eyes were uncharacteristically wide and white, a sign he was perturbed and annoyed. Goose was the same. He laid his ears back and bared his teeth to bite each time Eldon danced too close. Mags understood. She also wanted to bite Eldon and shut him up. She cooed to the horses and did her best to settle them, then she turned to Eldon. "I suggest you help the big kid with firewood. And we're not partners."

Eldon didn't follow instructions. "What do you mean, not partners, of course we are. Cut us in and we'll be great—"

"Before I met you, I had a sure bounty, was on my way back south, and not indebted to some dummy upstart Norrik goon. Because of you I not only lost my bounty, but now I gotta do a job I have no desire to do and can't get out of. So, we're not partners. You owe me. A lot. Now get to work."

"What do you mean a contract you can't get out of?" Ava asked. "You could just ditch all this and go south. Angmere won't follow you. Just don't come back this way."

"It doesn't work that way," Mags said. She didn't know these kids yet. How would they react if they knew Matchi had marked them for death if Mags couldn't find the bounty? She kept all the details to herself and gave them the most honest explanation she thought she could. "I'm contracted. If I break that, I won't be able to get work. Nobody wants to hire someone who may or may not do the job."

"Seems to me everyone hires someone who may or may not do the job." Ava shrugged. "That's why you better just do things yourself."

Mags felt her face grow hot and her brain spun trying to balance the notion that Ava was mostly correct with the fact that Mags didn't want her to be because it didn't fit with her situation. She finally pursed her lips together and gave a half-baked retort. "You just can't do things that way and get along. You'll understand when you're older."

"If I had a Crown for every time I heard that crap, I could

buy an island in the Paradisals. And how would you know so much? You're not older than us, although you act like a crotchety old lady." Ava scoffed at her.

"Oh, I'm plenty older than you. And smarter because I'm not the one who went messing with Norrikmen. Rouslanders should know better."

Ava jumped up and narrowed her eyes. She tensed up and Mags recognized the girl was ready to fight. "Keep telling me what Rouslanders should know and see how you like it."

"Calm down, kid. I didn't disparage anyone. But everyone knows how Norrikmen are and what they think of Rousland. It's smarter to steer clear of them. That's all," Mags said.

Ava still bristled but Dane intervened. He took Ava's arm. "Hey. Forget it. She didn't mean it how—"

Ava jerked her arm away and glowered at him. "You don't need to tell me anything either."

"Ava." Dane's deep voice was kind and rumbling and the girl's name sounded soothing the way he said it. It seemed to calm her for a second, then she fought it like a baby fighting sleep and huffed herself up again before storming off through the brush.

"She's volatile," Mags said.

"You have no idea," Eldon said.

Dane sighed. "Sometimes, yes. Rousland is a sore subject."

"I'll do my best to remember that," Mags said.

Dane nodded. "I'll get more firewood," he said, then he ambled off.

"So seriously, what's our plan?" Eldon said. He had plopped back down on the log.

"You're persistent," Mags said. She moved on to grooming Goose and when Dane returned with more wood, he asked if he could help with the horses.

"Nobody grooms them but me. Or rides them. Try it and you'll regret it." She eyed Dane suspiciously.

Dane held out a palm to Goose.

"He'll bite you," Mags warned.

Goose didn't bite. He pressed his soft nose into Dane's hand and affectionately lipped it.

"I wish I had a carrot," Dane said.

Mags felt a bit of jealousy flare. "Well, don't say I didn't warn you."

Eldon approached Duck. "I'll ride one. Maybe this black one. Whoa!" He jumped back just in time as Duck tried to bite a hunk out of him. "That horse is nuts!"

Mag's faith in her horses was restored. Even though Goose was still allowing Dane to pet him. She smiled and patted Duck. "You've been warned twice now."

Once Mags finished grooming the horses, she took them to the river to let them drink and fed them. After that, she went through her supplies and gear. She had rations for two people, but not four. That wasn't a big deal. There were plenty of places to pick up supplies between here and the coast, but as she went through her money, she confirmed she wasn't exactly rolling in coin. She'd been counting on Bog's bounty to replenish her coffers, so, losing that income was a problem. Not one that couldn't be overcome, but a problem none the less. She didn't just need coin for supplies. She'd also need coin for information. She only had a vague description of the women and they had a head start. She'd need to rely on information from anyone who'd seen them as well as her intuition and knowledge of the trails and travel routes. Her tracking skills wouldn't be of much use in such heavily traveled country, so the less she had to spend on feeding people and equipping them, the better.

Mags pulled a basic fishing line and hook set from her gear. "Can any of you fish?"

Eldon scoffed. "Look, we're not your servants. If you think we're going to do all the heavy lifting while you pet horses and give orders—"

"I'll do it. Do you have more than one set?" Dane took the fishing gear from her. "I can put out a few lines and maybe we can have breakfast too."

Mags gave him a little smile and nod. He wasn't such an idiot, maybe. She actually had two extra sets and passive fishing was an excellent idea. He took the gear and headed off for the river. She turned her attention to Eldon.

"Everyone has a job to do. Just out of curiosity, what do you see as your job?"

Eldon adopted a lax pose on the log and smirked. "I'm the brains, sweetheart."

"Don't call me sweetheart if you value your tongue, and no, you aren't. What else you got?"

His face reddened. "I'm a master negotiator. I do all the talking. I can talk anyone out of anything."

"No, you can't. Anything else?"

"No lock can keep me out."

"I highly doubt it."

"I can pick your pocket before you even know you have a coin." He held up his hands and twirled his fingers. "Magic."

"Pick my pocket then."

Eldon laughed. "Come on, sweet . . . " He caught himself. "I can't just do it while you're waiting for it."

"If you were as good as you say you are, you could." Mags shrugged. "Alright, Flea. Here's the deal. If you can pick my pocket while I finish up camp, then you eat tonight. If you can't, well, maybe you can talk a fish onto a hook."

She left him to ponder his attack and went to have a walk around the camp. A careful examination of the sky told her that weather wouldn't be a concern. It would be a chilly night in the North, which even in the summer was cold to Mags, native of the South that she was, but the sky was clear so she didn't worry about rain.

The perimeter was clear. She didn't see anything in the

65

tracks that concerned her. She found Ava examining a spot that was a perfect place to spy. The girl examined the bush and pointed to a hollowed-out space within it.

Mags nodded and pulled one of her long knives from the sheath at her back. She hacked off a few strategic branches from the front, ones that would make the bush less convenient for spying.

"Good catch," she said to Ava. "So, what's your story, kid? You and your brother recruited the big guy for muscle and started a gang?"

"You should be dead," the girl said, her voice even and quiet. There wasn't malice in it or even wonder. It was emotionless and factual.

"Like I said before, many times over," Mags replied.

"How is that possible?"

"It's not, yet here we are. I heal quickly." Mags scanned the rest of the area and spotted some edible berries. She picked them and Ava helped. "Why did you all think it was a good idea to mess with Norrik goons?"

"Just trying to make a living," Ava said. "Same as you."

"Norrikmen aren't known for loving your people," Mags said. "That seems like a poor career choice."

"Norrikmen aren't known for loving anyone, most of the time not even other Norrikmen," Ava said. "You got a problem with Rouslanders?" She puffed up.

"I don't have a problem with anyone. Except the Tyrraneans," Mags said.

Ava nodded. "Who's doesn't?" She paused a second then looked at the ground. "I wasn't aiming to kill you," Ava said.

"Oh, I know." Mags smiled and winked at the girl.

"Because if I had been aiming, I would have." The girl puffed up a bit more and scowled.

Mags stared at her a moment, to let her know she knew the

girl was posturing. "But you weren't. So here we are. Life is short. Friendly advice, kid, always aim."

She left Ava at the berry patch and headed back to camp. When she got back, Eldon had built a fire and Dane had returned from the river with three sprunt.

"If you have a knife I can borrow, I'll clean them," Dane offered.

"I'll do it. You hack at them and we lose half," Ava said as she walked into camp and dumped her berries.

"None of you carry knives?" Mags asked.

All three shrugged. Ava spoke up. "We left our weapons at the other camp."

Mags had examined their weapons left at that camp. They had one functional crossbow and a couple of poor swords. "Not weapons. Personal knives." Mags pulled a lean blade from one of her saddle bags. It wasn't a fighting knife, but a multi-purpose camp knife, good for chopping and slicing. She handed it to Ava. "Any knife is a weapon, but you should carry something to survive with. Swords aren't really practical in most cases."

Dane looked at his feet. "We don't really know—"

"Shut up, Dane! We know how to use them," Ava said. "I do anyway."

"Are you as good with a sword as you are with a crossbow?" Mags scoffed. "So let's just stop all the bullshit, right now. You guys are not trained fighters or mercs. No more pretending. It will get you killed and now, it may be a problem for me, so let's just move on."

"Why bother?" Ava asked. She crossed her arms and stared at Mags, a defiant, angry look on her face.

"Why bother with what?" Mags asked.

"Why bother with us at all? I mean if we're so useless and stupid. Why save us? If you're so much better than us at everything, why complicate life?" Ava threw the knife at Mags. It landed within a quarter of an inch from Mags's left boot.

Mags looked at the knife and raised an eyebrow. She pulled it from the ground. "It just seemed like the right thing to do. I've learned not to ignore that feeling." She chose her words carefully. She wasn't really ready to disclose a voice in her head told her to save them.

The voice chose that moment to speak up. *"No."*

Mags ignored it and flung the knife back at Ava. It hit the fish in the eyeball.

"Alright, so saving us is one thing. You got us away from that piece of shit Angmere. Thanks. Why keep us around? Has it always been your dream to start an academy for youth? You don't need to instruct us about personal knives and camp work and ambush bushes." Ava snatched the knife and flicked it at Mags. Again, it landed a hair's breadth from Mags's toe. "We'll be on our way."

"Like I said, you jagaloons cost me a bounty. I know you don't have coin enough to make up for that. Second, I gotta deal with this forced bounty and since I have to and I'm poorer for knowing you, you're going to help me." Mags grabbed the knife and threw it back at Ava. It whizzed by the girl's cheek, grazing it, and stuck in the tree beside her.

Ava's face reddened and she lifted her hand to touch her cheek. She wiped a trickle of blood away, pulled the knife from the tree and threw it directly at Mags's face.

Mags reached up and plucked the knife from the air, then in one motion, threw it back. It stuck in the fish again.

"Well, it's good to know you can throw a knife. When we get to the next trading post, let's get you some daggers."

She felt Eldon bump into her. As his hand reached into her pocket, she grabbed it and bent it back. Eldon squawked in pain.

"Clumsy. Do you really think that's going to work?" She let go of him and shoved him away.

He rubbed his wrist, then grinned at her. "I don't know. Maybe check your other pocket."

Mags rolled her eyes. She kept nothing in that pocket but just as she was about to call his bluff, she reached in and felt something. She pulled out a small, round pebble.

She gave him a grudging smile and a nod. "Not bad. See if you can do it next time without bumping me."

Mags sat down next to the fire and began cleaning her batons. She jumped when the Voice began singing. *"Evening shades are falling . . . time to go to rest . . . stars are softly calling . . . darling to her nest . . . pleasant dreams of bliss, love . . ."*

It wasn't a lullaby of the south, where Mags was from, but she had heard it before, in Rousland and certain areas of Arlea. She looked around at the Trio. None of them seemed to have heard it. Mags went back to her task.

Ava gutted the fish, spitted them and set them on the fire. Eldon and Dane went to look for more firewood. The horses nickered contentedly as they ate. Maybe the jagaloons weren't so useless after all.

CHAPTER
THIRTEEN

They reached the forks and what once was the bustling trade town of Calen in a relatively short amount of travel time considering the three people on foot, but in fact, it was the longest trip that Mags could remember in quite some time. Considering how far back Mag's memories went, that was saying something. Eldon jabbered non-stop from the moment he woke up until the moment he went to sleep each night. His sister and Dane seemed immune to it; Mags supposed that was how family worked—you just got really good at ignoring annoying behavior. But to her—one who spent most of her time alone, often going weeks at a time barely uttering anything aloud—it was not something she could ignore.

She pulled up Duck on the outskirts of Calen, dismounted and calmed herself.

"Alright. We have two tasks here in Calen. One is to get information. We need to pick up the trail of these two women."

"Can't you track them?" Dane asked.

"No. I saw nothing on the way here. It's a heavily traveled trade route and they seem smart enough to stay on it. It hides tracks. If they went off trail, that would certainly be easier. But the problem with using a heavy trade route is that two women traveling alone, especially a big one, will attract attention. People will remember them and for the right amount of money, they'll tell us." Mags held up the bag of coins. "Which brings us to the second thing we're after, which is more money."

Eldon clapped his hands and grinned. "No problem! I can steal—"

"No. No stealing. We don't need trouble." Mags glared at him. "I can almost always pick up work in towns and I know some people in Calen. The Villein is an old friend. We'll earn what we need."

"That's the long way around this. Aren't we on a deadline?" Ava said. "Maybe people can just remember or else."

"Okay. Listen. We're not stealing and we're not beating people up for information or money. We'll do this my way," Mags said.

"It's your ass," Ava said, looking bored and resigned.

Except it wasn't her ass. Mags would be fine physically. The Trio would pay the price if she ran out of time, only she couldn't bring herself to tell them that.

"Doesn't matter whose ass it is, this is what we're doing. We'll look around, keep a low profile." She pointed at Eldon. "That means don't do anything stupid and keep your mouth shut."

"Hey! I'm not a baby! You don't have to tell me how to—"

He yelped when Mags grabbed his ear and gave it a yank. "I will gag you and tie you up if I have to." She nodded at Dane. "You can handle this?"

Dane signed and took Eldon's arm. "I'll do my best."

"We'll check the outer community camp first." Mags moved off down the road toward the travelers' camp.

She needed a moment to think. She had a description of the quarry. Small blonde woman in the company of another blonde woman, but freakishly large. The small blonde would be

71

common enough in these northern parts. She would be more conspicuous the further south they went, but still, common enough to elude notice. Freakishly large on the other hand, man or woman, would be uncommon anywhere except maybe the Troll Coast. Whether the woman was a warrior or not, Mags didn't know, but as a fairly tall woman herself, although not freakishly so, she could say size generally lent itself to combat. Unless the second woman was a farmer, then she was a warrior of some sort, even if Angmere hadn't given her any respect for it.

No seasoned warrior on the run from Norrik goons would stroll into any town, especially not a trade town on the confluence of rivers and flash that around. Unless they were very, very stupid. Which didn't make sense since the duo had enough brainpower to get away from Angmere.

They found the camp on the south side of town. The place was of modest size, larger than most, but that made sense as Calen was a river port. It was late in the morning so the camp was mostly empty, the majority of travelers having moved on early. Mags counted three small groups. One was a two-man crew. She spotted them for mercs right away, and not good mercs. Their armor lay in untidy piles and their weapons haphazardly littered the area around their sleeping rolls. She'd seen men like them a thousand times. They bounced from company to company, and eventually became bushwhackers because no decent company would take them. The men were dirty and one of them snored loudly at nearly mid-day—drunks most likely.

She might have missed it if he hadn't itched his nose, but the second man was awake and staring at her. The movement of his hand was what caught her eye. The man had a long, thin nose and scraggly mustache. His eyes were short spaced apart and mean. Mags didn't let her eyes linger on him. She moved on but kept him in mind.

72

The second group was a family made up of a man, a woman, and three small children. They also had a tired looking donkey burdened with a few possessions and meager supplies. The whole family looked thin and under-fed and their clothes were worn. Possibly refugees. All of the children had a cough and runny noses and the mother, who was very pregnant, hobbled around the camp.

The third group of people were not travelers, but a husband and wife who seemed to be the camp bosses. This was not uncommon. Mags had encountered such people many times. Many of these camps had people paid to collect fees and keep order. Sometimes the people were the owners of the camp, and sometimes they were vassals of another. This team looked shifty. The woman was round and red and loud, the man nearly identical except for the loud. The woman did all of the talking. They were currently engaged with the father of the poor family.

"Please"—he held up his hands to the round woman—"my wife can't move on. Not right now. We need a few more days. We-we could work around the camp. I can chop wood; the children can clean. Please."

"None of that is our affair. You can't pay, move on. Go sleep in a field. But if you don't move out in the next hour or pay me, I'll have the Villein move all of you out." The woman peeled an apple and popped a slice into her mouth then chewed loudly.

The father looked defeated. His wife was on the verge of tears too, and her tight, round belly told Mags she was about to birth a baby any day. Of course, they couldn't move.

The loud red-faced woman looked up at Mags. "Help you?"

"I don't think you know what that word means, but we'll see. What are your rates?" Mags asked.

"Two a night. That's the space. An extra for the well and the firepit."

They were riverside. Mags wondered what well the woman spoke of. "Two bronze?" Mags asked.

"Two copper."

Mags laughed out loud. "For that I could stay in an inn. For a month."

"Then take yer coin and go stay in one. Won't likely be here. I'd like to see the inn you could get these days for that." The woman huffed and shoved another slice of apple in her mouth.

"Why would I pay to stay here when there's free water in the river right there and I can camp anywhere along it I like?" Mags asked.

"'Cause you can't. That's the new law. We don't need no more immigrants and wastes taking up space here. Villein runs out anybody who can't pay. And good luck to you if you move on. Roads are rough these days."

"Real rough these days." The fat man spat his words and glob of tobacco at Mag's foot.

"Roads are rough all the time," Mags said. She didn't recall Calen being such an inhospitable place, and her friend, Emile Book, the Villein, wouldn't run anyone out for being poor. But to be fair, she hadn't been this way in a while. War did things to people and this area had been hit hard. Travel and trade suffered. That meant Calen suffered.

"I was supposed to meet a party here." She looked around the camp, pretending she hadn't marked all of them the second she stepped in. "Doesn't look like they're here yet. Were you full up last night?"

"That kind of answer ain't free." The woman shook her head and pursed her lips.

Mags pulled a copper coin from her bag. "Were you full?"

"Nope," the woman said. She held out her palm for the coin. "That won't get you much."

"Yes, I can see that," Mags said. She turned from the red-faced couple to the father. "How long have you been here?"

"Four days."

"I'm hoping I didn't miss my friends. Two women. One of

them kind of big. They were supposed to wait for me here but I got waylaid up north and I'm worried I may have missed them."

The man nodded. "I think you did. There was a big woman here three days ago. She was kind to my wife and girls. We shared the fire and some stew. I didn't see another woman though."

"Yes, that sounds like her." Mags smiled. She pretended not to notice the informative bit about there being only one woman, but splitting up in towns and camps was smart. That didn't bode well for tracking. "Well, I guess I'll catch up with them next port up. We were all going to take a barge down together. Maybe they'll get off in Rockport and wait for me." She nodded toward the camp keepers. "I can see why they didn't want to stay here."

The man nodded. "Yes. No real choice for us."

"When is your baby due?" Mags asked.

"My wife says any day now. I-I was hoping we could make it to my family in Darjin but I don't think we're going to."

Mags smiled at him. "No. I don't think you will be able to make it before then." She handed him a stack of bronze coins. "Thank you for helping me. You know, I used to know a stableman here. He would let me sleep in the livery. I'll send word back if I can help you."

The man flushed and stared at the money. "That's very generous. I-I can't take it." He thrust the money back at her.

Mags refused to take it back. "No. Get your family some place more hospitable."

"Are you really going to give him that much money? If we're already short—" Ava whispered in her ear.

Mags held up a hand and stopped her. "I'll figure it out."

"You make no sense," Ava backed off and crossed her arms. She wasn't the only one angry at Mag's generosity.

"You can't just give him money when I was telling you—"

the red-faced woman screeched and got close enough for Mags to smell apple and rot on her breath.

"I can give my money to anyone I like," Mags said. "And you weren't telling me squat. Now get out of my face."

"I'll have the Villein on you!" the woman screamed and pointed a finger at Mags.

"For what? Giving away my own money?" Mags laughed.

"For aiding these Rousland refugees. We don't put up with that here! They take our food and never pay. And they cause crime! They're all murderers and thieves! The new Villein will hear about this."

Ava stepped forward and snarled at the woman. Mags grabbed her and hauled her back before addressing the fat woman.

"Well, I guess I've seen enough to never underestimate anyone, but I think these people just need a safe place for a bit and they'll be on their way. Anyway, they can pay now, so I'm not sure why you're screaming. I think it's in your best interest to shut up." Mags glared down at the woman. Her blue hand began to itch and throb. The woman saw it and immediately took three big steps back.

"Just get out of here. We don't want any trouble."

Mags smiled. "Something we can all agree on." She bowed slightly to the woman and nodded at the little family. "Thank you all for your help."

"Is that how you keep a low profile?" Ava asked.

Mags ignored her. They were now almost out of money. She would have to grab a bounty or two. That was usually easy enough in a port town. But then again, Calen had changed. If this post-war town was more capitalistic that might not work so well for her. On the other hand, assholes loved bounties, so she'd just have to see.

CHAPTER
FOURTEEN

Calen was much less crowded than she remembered it. River port towns were rough but populous and busy. The war hadn't helped but it was over now. Time to get things moving again. But prosperity hadn't returned. The buildings were rundown and showed scars from fires, maybe from battle, maybe from raids. The people moved about more slowly than they normally did in port, almost as if they were afraid to make noise or attract attention. That seemed odd. Not how she remembered Calen at all.

Raylon Canter had run the general trade store for years. Raylon and his wife Fallon were kind souls. They had always been happy to share meals with Mags and help her in any way they could when she was in town. If she was low on coin, Raylon gave her good deals on supplies and Fallon always pressed food for the road into her hands as she left town. In return, Mags did whatever she could to help them—painting, maintenance work on the store, or whatever they needed done. She would start there, not only because she missed her friends, but also because Raylon and Fallon knew everyone and everything that went on in Calen. They would help.

When Mags stopped in front of the store, her heart sank. The property was as faded and rundown as everything that surrounded it. One window was boarded up and the normally neat whitewash peeled and flaked off all around the exterior walls. When she went inside, the shelves were only minimally stocked with goods. Fallon stood behind the counter. The woman's face looked tired and gray. Worry and sadness lived there. Fallon's eyes lit up when she saw Mags and she dared a smile, but it faded when a tall thin man came out of the backroom—a man who wasn't Raylon. Fallon looked at him and winced, like a dog who anticipated a blow.

Mags felt her face flush and the place on her cheek burn. She breathed in deep and attempted to get to the bottom of the mystery. "Hello, Fallon. It's good to see you again."

Before Fallon could answer, the man interrupted, "What do you want?"

Mags cocked her head and regarded him for a second before answering. "That doesn't seem to be good customer service."

"Customers pay." He looked Mags and the Trio over. "Can you pay?"

"Well, we do know what stores are so we understand you don't loan food and goods," Mags answered. She looked to Fallon. "Where's Ray?"

Fallon shook her head but didn't answer. The man glared at her. "You don't speak to her. I'm running things now. The geezer who owned this place couldn't pay his taxes. He's where all degenerates go. The Stocks. Now what do you want? I haven't got all day."

Her blue hand itched and the red mark on her face burned hotter, but she controlled all of that. Fallon was afraid and Mags didn't want to make trouble before she knew more and could correct it. She looked to Fallon and smiled at her, hoping she conveyed the fact that she would help. Fallon caught the look and smiled back before she moved off to dust something on the back shelves.

Mags turned back to the man and exhaled, then asked politely, "Blankets please."

He snapped his fingers at Fallon, who jumped, but quickly produced a wool blanket and handed it to him. He slammed it down on the counter. "Seventy-five bronze."

"Are you kidding? There's no way—" Ava yelled at him.

Mags patted her shoulder. "That's kind of high, no?"

"Prices are what they are. Pay them or get out."

"Not many can pay that," Dane said.

"Not our problem," the goon said. He looked to Mags. "Pay it or don't."

"Indeed," Mags said through clenched teeth. "I'll be back." The statement was for Fallon, not the goon. She bowed slightly to him, then ushered the Trio out.

"There's no way anyone can afford to live here," Dane said when they got outside.

"Something is definitely wrong," Mags said. She grabbed the horses' reins and headed off down the street. Calen was more problematic than she had anticipated.

Mags walked down the main street. She easily found the livery stable. Just like the trading post, it was weathered and needed a coat of wash, but the familiar sign of her old friend Elio Anton still hung outside. Mags entered and saw the stable was clean, Elio's normal standard, but was empty save for one animal, a large white hunter. He laid his ears straight back as she approached and slammed around in his stall, wary and agitated. His big eyes rolled back in his head and warned her to back off.

"Easy. I won't hurt you." Mags held out a hand to him and hummed an old song. In a few seconds, he relaxed enough for her to put her hands on him. He was big and fed properly, but a close inspection showed scars on his back from whipping and at his mouth where someone had yanked hard on his bit.

Anger boiled inside her, but Mags calmed herself. Elio wouldn't treat an animal roughly, so she knew it wasn't his horse. Mags patted the big white and rubbed his muzzle. "We'll see if we don't sort you out." She pulled a carrot from Elio's feed bin and broke it up, then fed it to him. "Where's old Elio? At his forge, I suppose?"

The horse grunted at her as he chomped his carrots. She gave him a last pat and went off in search of Elio.

Mags found him at his forge as she predicted, but he wasn't alone. He had an apprentice—a boy of about fourteen. The boy's hammering was slow, but steady and Elio nodded approvingly as they worked.

"Good. You'll get stronger. Easy. Steady. Careful. Power and speed will come." He looked up when Mags approached and gave her a smile. "It's been a long time, Magdalena."

"I suppose so." She grinned back at him and shook his hand. "How are you?"

"Old and tired," Elio said. He stretched his back.

"Yes. Same," Mags replied.

Elio laughed. "You don't look it."

"I feel old and tired, anyway." She nodded to the boy. "So you finally got an apprentice."

"Hard to come by when there's coin to be made fighting. That's the only trade most know these days."

Mags nodded. "It's a short tenure when fighting is your trade, even if you're good. Especially if you're good. The fights seem to find you." The pair of them walked out front.

"You working?" Elio asked.

"Always," Mags said. "Looking for two women. Blonde, both of them and one of them big."

"Haven't seen them. At least I can tell you they didn't come in here. You can try the two taverns, but unless they're flush with coin, they would have had to skip them."

"Yes," Mags said. "I know the war hit hard here, but prices are high and this place isn't bustling."

Elio nodded. "New Villein. He says he's cleaning up the riff raff, but his solution to crowding was to raise taxes and use goons to beat up anyone who disagrees or can't pay."

"Seems like a poor businessman but that problem usually rights itself." Mags sat down on a bench and Elio sat beside her.

"Usually, but this fellow, he's got something going here. He charges all the merchants heavy taxes. Even taxes everyone on Market Day. Raylon? Villein sent his men in the store. They claimed they found him withholding. Took over his store, threw Ray in the stocks. Most folks are in trouble. I keep my head down and pay. Best way. It's getting harder though."

"I can see that." The rage percolated in her gut. When Elio clucked at her, she knew her face showed her anger.

"We'll weather it, Magdalena," he said.

"I didn't say anything," Mags said.

"You don't have to," Elio said.

"I'm looking for two women and work, so I'll go see what's up with this guy. Maybe he has some bounties."

"No jobs that would suit you," Elio said. "For a bounty hunter, you're a bit particular. And anyway, he taxes the bounties."

Mags shrugged. "I prefer discerning. Look. I was at the outskirt camp and I met a family. The wife was pregnant, gonna bust any day, and they can't travel. That camp matron was charging a fortune. You think you could help them out until they can be mobile?"

"That could be a while, Magdalena. If the woman is going to—"

"Yes. I know, but they need help. Come on, do it for me. You owe me one, remember? That big idiot that tried to run you through with the pitchfork?"

"Because you stole his horse."

"I liberated his horse. He beat it. I didn't steal it. Besides, he had a warrant in Coldspine. Stealing doesn't count in that case."

"Oh really?" Elio laughed. "They have children you say?"

"Three little ones."

"You're going to cause me trouble for sure," Elio said, "but alright, I'll take Pugio and collect them."

"Great! I knew I could count on you. Oh, umm, by the way, whose horse is that?" Mags nodded at the white.

"Magdalena. Don't."

"Hey. Just asking."

"Flashy guy, gambler. Likely in the tavern. Also seems like a cutthroat. I doubt you can miss him. He has a gold tooth."

"Classy. Alright."

Elio nodded to the Trio and raised an eyebrow at Magdalena. "You have friends?"

"Long story." Mags hesitated for a second, looked to Dane, then handed the reins to Elio. "I'm going to see this Villein."

"He's nobody to mess around with, Mags," Elio said.

"Hey, Elio. I'm a professional. What could I possibly do to irritate a villein? I help the law."

"Well, you're gonna do what you're gonna do. That much I know, just watch your step. There's worse things than horse apples around here."

"That's everywhere," Mags said, winking at him as she left the stable.

"Sounds like this Villein and his dummies need a lesson," Ava huffed. She crossed her arms over her chest.

"That's a fact, but right now I want to find my friend," Mags said as she headed off toward the Villein's place. When she found it, she went directly to a set of stocks occupied by a small man, thin, clothed in dirty rags, and barely conscious. Mags knelt beside him and tipped his chin up. His eyes were glazed and he felt hot with fever. When he finally focused on her, he smiled. "I dreamed you'd come."

"Raylon, I'm going to . . ." Mags nearly cried. She kept the tears in check and looked at the lock that held the stocks closed around Raylon's wrists.

The old man shook his head. "No. Too late. Help Fallon. Please."

"I'll help you both," Mags said. She kissed the old man's forehead. His skin burned her lips he was so feverish. He wouldn't survive much longer. Mags stood up. She addressed the Trio. "Stay here. I'm going to go talk to this Villein." She looked to Dane. "Don't let anyone hurt him," she said.

Dane nodded. Ava and Eldon formed a sort of protective half-circle around the old man and for a second, Mags felt something for them. She nodded her approval, then squared her shoulders and ascended the steps that led to the office, a grim and determined look on her face that in over three hundred years, had rarely boded well for anyone, especially her.

FIFTEEN

The Villein's office was more opulent than Mags remembered Book's being. The new Villein fancied a huge mahogany desk that took up a good portion of the room and it was raised up high on a platform lending a lordly loft to anyone who sat there. It reminded her of the set up in Angmere's feast hall, like that of someone pretending to be more important than they were.

He lounged in a throne-like chair with a high back and ornate carvings, yet wore simple clothes, functional black leathers, which told her he was no stranger to fighting. The Villein smiled at her as he assessed her. The smile was meant to look friendly and smooth, but Mags knew a cruel predator when she saw one and there was no humanity in those eyes. This man was dangerous.

"You're the new Villein?" Mags asked.

Before he could answer, she heard a throat clearing behind her. She turned and saw a short man with a ledger and a pencil, which he held up as if to summon her.

"This is Villein Kassun. I am his assistant, Petri. We must inform you that all bounty hunters, mercenaries, and refugees

84

must register at the outer camp and remain there until we grant a pass to enter Calen proper."

"How do you know I'm any of those things?" Mags asked.

"Everyone in this country is one of those things." The Villein's voice was deep and rumbling.

"It might be helpful if you posted that sign somewhere," Mags said.

"We've just informed you. If you will not comply, then you will be apprehended and—"

"Easy, Pee," the Villein said. "It's a small mistake. Lots make it. We don't just go throwing people in stocks because they forget to check in and register." Kassun rose and came in front of the desk. He put his hand on the little man's shoulder. Instead of a fatherly gesture, his paw looked as if it pinned the little man in place and nearly buckled him under the strain. "Now normally, I would have to insist that you go on out to the south camp and register with Sal and Dee, but I heard you already stopped by there, so we'll just say you're registered and approved."

"That's great. I came to ask about a man in your stocks. His name is Raylon—"

"Raylon Canter owes back taxes," the little man interrupted.

"Well he can't pay you if he's dead," Mags said. She spoke directly to Kassun and ignored the little man.

"We will recover our money from his business. Canter will remain in the stocks as an example for oth—"

His words were cut off when Mags reached down with her blue hand and clamped it around his throat. Again, she spoke directly to Kassun. "I think your point has been made. Release him to me and I'll see his debt is paid."

Kassun kept smiling at her. She noticed his eyes went to her hand. They sparkled greedily and his smile twitched. "A test first. Bring us a man, his name is Ance Decker. His bounty should cover your friend's bail."

"Fine." Mags let go of Petri and he grabbed his throat and coughed. She ignored him. "I'll need a description."

"No need. You'll find him in one of the taverns. He's a gambler," Kassun said. "He won't be easy to miss."

"If that's the case, why don't you just go get him yourself?" Mags asked.

"Oh, you'll see," Kassun said. "Better hurry. That old man out front won't last the night."

Mags controlled the rage and gave him a curt nod before she turned and exited. When she got outside, her mood was further degraded. Eldon was missing.

"Alright, where is he?"

"He thinks he can get more coin," Ava said. "He went to one of the taverns to gamble."

"Bukker's Seventh Cock! This is all I need. Why didn't the two of you stop him? And what's he gambling with? He doesn't have any money." She looked to Dane and Ava.

Dane sighed and looked at his feet.

Ava shrugged. "He figures it out. Look, I gave up trying to stop him from stupid a long time ago," she said. "It'll go better for you if you do the same."

"His stupid affects us all," Mags said.

Ava nodded. "Oh I know. But Eldon is going to Eldon."

"Not for very much longer at this rate," Mags said as they headed off toward the taverns.

CHAPTER
SIXTEEN

The two taverns were directly across the street from one another. One of the inns, The Spotted Hound, looked decent. In this case, decent meant without any busted windows and the door was on its hinges. On the other hand, The Bashful Bollock across the street had no windows intact, the door hung crooked on one hinge, and an ancient woman wearing an entire pot of rouge and a threadbare red dress sat in the other window. Loud noises, screams, grunts, cheers, and breaking glass came from the inside. The Spotted Hound was quiet.

Mags looked heavenward, not because she trusted any deity to help her but more out of habit. "Please let him have gone in the quiet one where I likely won't get rabies." But in her heart, she knew where Eldon would go and it wasn't in the classy place.

"Watch yourself in here. The quicker we grab him and get out the better," Mags said. She squared her shoulders and turned toward the door.

"Aye, you're a tall, dark, handsome one," the crone in the window cackled at her. The old woman's eyes were so cloudy with age Mags figured all she could get right was the tall and dark part of anyone. She ignored the woman and entered the tavern.

It smelled as pleasant as it looked—like piss and body odor and stale ale. The barman wore an eyepatch and smiled a toothless smile at her. Another old prostitute tottered up to her. Mags stepped away. Miscreants of every size and shape drank at the bar, most of them looked like the out of work merc she spied back at the camp. Eldon was not among them. He was however, among a group of men seated at a grimy table throwing dice.

Mags felt her face grow hot. Nothing but trouble came of gambling and only disaster came of gambling with no money— which was what Eldon had.

"Great. Just great," Ava said. "I guarantee he's cheating."

"But he hides it so well," Mags said as she rolled her eyes and walked over to the table.

"So yeah, I told Angmere we'd find this broad easy, but we'd do it for no less than a hundred copper. Half now, half on delivery." Eldon puffed up. He blew on his dice and let them go.

"Whew! Seven again! Where are we at now? Twenty?"

"Nobody is that lucky," a fat man in stained leathers growled. He spat on the floor and glared at Eldon.

"I mean, they're not even my dice, how could I cheat?" Eldon said.

Mags cringed. "Never bring up cheating when you're cheating," Mags said to Ava.

The girl nodded. "He thinks if you say what they're thinking it throws them off you. Yeah, we know he's wrong. We've tried to tell him."

"Too bad this lesson's going to get all of us stabbed," Mags said.

In addition to Eldon and a fat man, there was another. The third man was tall and slick-looking. Not literally greasy, he was tidy in his appearance, but slimy no doubt, as if all the baths in the world couldn't wash away his ick. He wore rings on every finger and a gold tooth shone from his mouth. Mags felt a flicker of anger flash through her and she gritted her teeth as she surmised this was the owner of the abused horse she'd found at Elio's stable.

"Easy there, Fatty," he said to the big man. "The kid is right. They're my dice so how could he cheat?"

Mags nearly laughed but kept quiet. The dice were almost certainly loaded and Eldon, being the smarmy little shit he was, must have been quite adept at figuring out the throw.

"See? He's even saying it. I can't cheat. They're his dice," Elson said. When he looked up and caught sight of Mags and Ava, he gulped and his face went white. "Well, chaps, looks like it's time for me to go. I-I have to see to my men and we really have to hit the trail, you know, find our quarry, run it to ground. You know how it is."

"Don't be silly. You just got here and anyway; you have to give us a chance to win our money back." The slick man motioned to the barkeep. "A round of ale for my fellows here." He finally noticed Mags. He stood up, bowed, then kissed her hand. Mags held back her disgust. "What a lucky day to see such a beauty in a place such as this."

"How gentlemanly, but I'm afraid I'm only here to collect my acquaintance and get moving." Mags motioned to Eldon. "Time to go, chief."

"What? No! Stay! All of you." The slick man looked to her and Ava. He smiled and took her hand. Mags clenched her other hand as it tingled. She would never feel clean again. "My name is Ance Decker and I would be absolutely honored if you, beautiful lady, would join us. Please?"

This was the man Kassun wanted. Mags put it all together. Ance was a killer. She wagered he had many knives on him and he would stick them in you so fast you'd be dead before you could count them all. Kassun wasn't dumb. If Mags could bring

Ance back, Kassun won. If Ance gutted Mags, Kassun won. The anger boiled in her even more. She didn't believe she could bear for Kassun to win. Her play would be to get Eldon and Ava clear, then go for Ance. She could take a stabbing. Eldon and Ava, not so much.

"I'm sorry, but I'm not much into gambling," Mags said. "And really, we're on a tight schedule."

"Oldam hates a tight schedule. Or does he love it? I don't know." Ance laughed at his poor innuendo.

"Who does?" Mags said. She didn't laugh at all.

"Really, I insist." Ance motioned toward the empty seat. The other hand rubbed a large, silver-hilted knife at his belt. The goons ringing him growled and shifted on their feet.

Mags smiled, then sighed. "Okay, but we really can't stay long." She sat down at the table and glared at Eldon. "I sure hope we don't break your lucky streak."

Ance laughed. "How could you be anything but good luck?"

"Opinions are varied." Mags looked at the stack of coins Eldon had amassed. It was significant. He picked up a coin and flipped it across his knuckles and back. He grinned at her but Mags didn't return the smile. In fact, she glared harder. Eldon lost the grin and put the coin back in the pile. He gave a cough, then picked up the dice. He rolled four.

"What? Not a seven? How'd that happen?" Ance laughed and slapped the table. "Maybe you're lucky for me." He winked at Mags.

"Ok, umm, well, let me roll again. Umm . . . okay eight. Whew." Eldon scooped up the dice and rolled in quick succession. He gave a good show and rolled three more times before he finally busted and rolled a seven.

"Yes! Thank Oldam! My turn!" Ance grabbed the dice and immediately rolled an eleven. "What do you know?" He smiled and pulled the pot of money toward him. "Blow on my dice?" He held his fist to Mags. She struggled to contain her disgust.

"I think you're doing fine without me." She plastered a fake smile on her face.

Ance rolled twice more, winning rolls each time. He pushed all of his hand in the pot. "Care to make it interesting?" He raised his eyebrows at Eldon. "One roll each. Highest takes all."

"No, I think we'd better go," she said as she went to stand up.

"Sure," Eldon said. He smiled and pushed all of his money in the pot.

"Excellent!" Ance scooped up the dice, blew on them, then made a show of shaking them. When he released them, he rolled an eleven. "How about that?" He sat back in his chair and clapped.

Mags stared long and hard at Eldon. "How about that. Gonna be hard to beat—"

She didn't even get the whole sentence out before Eldon grabbed the dice and rolled a twelve.

"Wow! Look at that!" He went to grab the money, but Ance stopped him.

"Yeah. What are the chances?" Ance wasn't smiling anymore. "You think I don't know you've been cheating? They're my dice."

"Cheating? How could I cheat? I just rolled." Eldon flailed his hands around and his face got red.

"Look, whatever, just keep all the money." Mags stood up and grabbed Eldon by the collar. "We're gonna go. Eldon, Ava, exit please."

"You're not going anywhere. This idiot scared away all the play and ruined my shot at this town. And that's all my money anyhow. I want everything you got." He pulled his knife and pointed it Eldon. "Now. Or I'll gut the both of you."

Mags looked heavenward. There were going to be a lot of stabbings. "I should let him gut you, you know," Mags said. In a smooth motion she pulled her batons, bashed Ance's knife hand and sent the blade flying.

Ance pulled another knife, a thin sliver from his boot and jammed it in Mag's side.

She barely winced, but the blood bloomed on her shirt. She reached out with her batons and cracked Ance right on the collar bone. He screamed and collapsed in a heap as his arms were useless. Mags ignored him. She pulled the dagger from her side and tossed it on the table.

Mags's shirt was done for. "That's the second shirt that's been ruined since I met you idiots," she said. She grabbed Ance by the hair and drug him toward the exit.

When Eldon didn't follow, she turned and looked to see him standing at the table, staring at her in disbelief. "What are you waiting on? Let's go."

He snapped out of it and stumbled around the table, tripping over himself.

Ava stopped him and pointed to the table. "Get the money, dummy."

Eldon scooped it into his hat and followed her out the door. "What are you going to do with him?" Eldon asked.

Mags started off down the street, dragging the cutthroat with her. "Get paid."

CHAPTER
SEVENTEEN

Mercifully, the Villein's office was not far away as neither Ance nor Eldon would have survived a long trek. Ance screamed non-stop, which Mags could understand as she wasn't interested in gently transporting him. As she drug him along, he bounced off wagon wheel ruts and rocks. Eldon, on the other hand, had no reason to talk non-stop, yet he did. It was worse than Ance's screams.

"What are you gonna do with him? Is he worth a lot? I get half, right? For spotting him. Do you think he'll be enough to get a horse? How much are they? Are there more people we can bag? Where did you learn to use those stick things?"

Mags stopped and turned to Eldon. "If you don't shut up, I'm going to use those sticks to break your jaw." She addressed Ava. "Go to the livery stable. Wait there for me."

Ava shook her head. "You can't just order me around."

"No way. I want to see what happens to him. I bet I can get us more money for him!" Eldon danced from foot to foot.

Mags let go of Ance. He collapsed in the mud and whined. She grabbed Eldon's shirt front and hauled him up off his feet.

"Keep your mouth shut. Even if this Villein wasn't touchy, which he is, you couldn't bargain. If you get the urge to say anything, anything at all, just think of life without a tongue. Because if you so much as exhale a loud breath, I will make a tongue-less future a reality for you. Do you understand?"

Eldon had the good sense to answer silently with a slow nod. Mags let him down and he fell backward into the street.

She stalked over to Ance, who had dragged himself down the street. She yanked him up and continued on to the Villein.

Kassun looked surprised to see Mags so soon, but the surprise turned to a smile when he saw Ance. Kassun had added muscle to his crew. Two goons, big and burly and armed, flanked him. They stared stoically at Mags.

"That was fast! I heard you were good, but this? This is impressive! Ance, do you have my money?" Kassun came from behind the desk.

"They-they took all my money. Beat me and took—"

Kassun nodded at one of the goons and the big man back-handed Ance with one of his huge paws. Ance fell coughing against the floor. Blood poured from his mouth and nose. Kassun smiled at Mags.

"So money. The bounty for this poor specimen is fifty copper," he said. "However, taxes, even at ten percent, bring that down to forty-five. Then there's the Bounty Hunter Registration fee, that's twenty-five copper. There's a toll of five copper per visitor, so for you that's fifteen."

"There's more of us than that. We'll show—ow!" Eldon shut up when Ava gave him a sharp elbow to the ribs.

"So that entitles you to five copper of the original bounty." Petri counted out five coins and held them up.

"Unfortunately, there is a fine for failing to properly register. That's fifty copper," Kassun nodded at Petri, who pulled the coins back and put them in his pile.

Mags sucked in a breath and smiled at them. "How interesting, that you didn't say anything about that before."

Petri cleared his throat. "Yes, well, that means you owe forty-five copper and clearly, you can't pay Canter's taxes. You and all of your companions will be detained until the amount is paid in full. You will work to pay the debt. And we will take possession of any horses or livestock you have," Petri said.

The Villein patted his assistant on the back. He grinned at Mags and his eyes sparkled with malicious, triumphant glee.

Mags met his eyes and smiled back. "Nobody is taking my horses."

She pulled her batons and in two solid whacks took down the goon at the door. "Run," she instructed Ava and Eldon, then she turned back to the other four men. Their shock at her quick, brutal treatment of their coworker wore off and they came for her. The big one from the left came first. Mags dropped to her knees and landed four blows to his kneecaps. He screamed and crumpled to the floor. The one from the right moved in next. Mags hammered at his shins and when he went down, she knocked him unconscious. She sprang to her feet. Kassun and Petri's mouths hung open, shocked at the speed with which Mags had lessened the advantage they held. Petri squeaked and ran behind the desk. Kassun's shock wore off and rage replaced it.

"You've made a big mistake," he said. He pulled a long dagger and stepped toward Mags.

"So many mistakes," Mags agreed. She hit his dagger hand. The bones cracked and he screamed and dropped the knife. In six quick blows from each of her batons, she broke his forearms, his upper arms and his collarbone in two places. He screamed again and dropped to his knees. Mags sheathed her batons and punched Kassun in the nose, then gave him an uppercut that knocked him out.

"Please. I just work for him. I-I was just doing my job," Petri stammered. He held his palms up and looked at his feet as he bowed his head.

"You should have picked a different job," Mags said. She knocked him out with a light blow.

"We should kill all of them. They'll just come after us." Ava and Eldon hadn't run. They had seen the whole fight. Ava drew her dagger.

"No," Mags tossed Petri to the side. "I don't kill anyone unless I have to, and I don't have to kill these people."

"Ava is right. That guy will put a bounty on us for sure. He'll send these guys," Eldon said.

"Nope. They won't go." Mags grabbed the conscious goon by his hair. "You're hired?" he grimaced and nodded. "And if you're not paid by this guy, you'll move on?" He nodded again. "Good. See that you do."

"What if there's more?" Ava asked.

"They all understand money. No money. No fighty." Mags yanked his hair again. "If you have any more in your company, I suggest you pass along the message that this gig is played out." He nodded and Mags let him go. "Now we're gonna need some rope."

"What for? He said they wouldn't leave," Eldon asked.

Mags kicked Kassun. "We're going to make a gift of a pig to the good people of Calen."

"And we'll take this." Eldon's eyes gleamed with delight as he rummaged through the money chest on the desk. He picked up a handful of coins and then let them go, smiling at the clinking noise they made as they hit each other. "There's hundreds here."

"That's not ours. It belongs to the people here in town he stole it from," Mags said. She found some rope and trussed up Kassun like a pig ready for roasting.

"You can't be serious. We're not going to leave all this money," Ava said. "We need weapons, supplies, horses."

"Take all the weapons off these guys. They're pros. It'll be good stuff. We'll make it to Sheaf." She closed the chest and locked it in one of the jail cells. She locked Kassun and Petri in the other. Mags took the keys and headed outside.

Dane stood watch beside Raylon. Mags unlocked the stocks and the man collapsed. Dane picked him up and they headed back to the store.

Mags quickly tossed the shop warden out on his ear. "I suggest you move on to another town," Mags said as the man held his broken arm and scrambled around in the dusty street. When she went back inside, she headed up the stairs that connected the store to the living quarters above. Dane had put Raylon in the bed and Fallon sobbed as she held his hand.

"Mags, he's sick. I-I don't think he'll make it." Fallon cried and Mags held her.

"Clean him up. We'll bring help." Mags kissed Fallon on the top of the head, then headed off to find the healer.

When she came down the stairs, she smelled rotten eggs.

"You're not needed, Torment."

He didn't take physical form but stayed in his green vapor state. His voice echoed from the putrid mist.

"Magdalena, he'll die. I can help him."

"So can the healer," Mags said. She wasn't desperate enough for Torment and his games.

"But that's not a sure thing," Torment said, his taunt a sing-song annoyance. "Why take the chance?"

"I don't have time for this. Go away."

The green mist swirled around her, surrounding Mags in the smell of rot. She gagged.

"It's so simple. You know I can make it all go away for him."

"I'm going to call Kohoc," Mags said.

"Fine." Torment pouted from the mist. "But if he dies, well, know you could have stopped it."

The green vapor swirled around her one last time, filling her nostrils with the smell of death. Torment laughed when Mags doubled over and vomited, then the mist dissipated, leaving her dry heaving.

CHAPTER
EIGHTEEN

Raylon was sick, but not beyond the skill of a good healer, although it was touchy for a few days. His fever raged and several times Mags thought about calling Torment and allowing him to torture her, but thankfully, it wasn't necessary. The healer declared him out of danger three days later.

Mags helped Elio and the rest of the townspeople of Calen sort out their Villein problem. As Mags predicted, once the money dried up, the mercs moved on. Mags gave a couple of them a little push as they fancied themselves just the men to fill the power vacuum left by Kassun. A few broken bones later, they thought otherwise and left town.

The townspeople elected a new Villein, a good and honest one, who kept them from killing the old one. In that, Kassun was lucky. Instead of drowning him outright, they covered him and Petri in tar, tied them together, and threw them in the river.

"Won't they drown?" Dane asked as they watched the two men bob and scream in the water.

"Their feet weren't tied," Mags said. The river carried them off. She felt no guilt at all. "So I'd say they at least have a sporting chance."

Four days after they arrived in Calen, they continued on with Ance bound and gagged on Goose. Mags was sure he would yield a bounty elsewhere. They were about an hour outside of town when Mags got a hinky feeling. She stopped and turned back toward the town. There was nobody on the road. That seemed strange to her. There should have been more people heading south and an equal number heading north, yet they were the only people on the road and it was already mid-morning. Not only were there no other travelers, but the forests were quiet as well. No little bird songs, no rustling in the underbrush, nothing. She didn't expect much in the way of nature noise as it was heavily traveled, but if the sparrows and finches were quiet, something was off. That something was almost always an ambush.

Duck and Goose grew restless. They were calm and solid animals, so if they didn't like the smell of something, neither did Mags.

Ava noticed something too. "Something isn't right."

Mags nodded. "Yeah. There's somebody skulking about."

She looked down the road and saw a curve. Mags pointed toward it. "I'd wager someone is waiting for us just around that bend."

Ava agreed. "Good place to ambush. What should we do?"

Mags handed the reins to Dane. "You guys keep walking. Slow. Steady. Chat like normal. I'll meet you around the bend."

"Maybe I should come with you, for stealth," Eldon said. Everyone looked at him and he turned red. "I'm stealthy."

"Actually, Eldon, it's critical you keep on the road. Lots of talk. Loud. They'll be listening. Dane, when trouble comes, drop their reins. They'll know what to do." Mags checked her weapons and headed off into the forest.

She swung way around but moved fast and silent through

the forest. When she thought she was far enough ahead to flank whoever was waiting on the road, she cut inward, then crept closer to the road.

It was a group of Norrikmen. She recognized them from Angmere's enclave as part of Ulf's crew. Ulf was not there, but she'd discern his whereabouts soon enough.

The Norrikmen were serious trouble. Numerically it was an even match, four on four, however even though Ava and Eldon liked to talk of prowess, Mags had yet to see then actually scrap and Dane was too gentle a soul to ever be a good fighter. The Norrikmen were seasoned raiders, skilled and nasty when it came to a fight. That gave them the advantage, and it doubled the advantage in an ambush.

She lay in the weeds to the side of the road and waited. Soon enough she heard Eldon's loud chatter. It carried easily around the bend. Mags grinned and the Norrikmen got ready.

"That little fucker never shuts up," one of the raiders said. He carried a war hammer and he readied it as the Trio rounded the bend.

Just as they came in sight, Mags dashed from the brush. She pulled her batons and went to work on the raider nearest her, breaking his knees, then hitting him in the throat. He fell into the road, clutching at his neck. As she moved on to the next, she gave a whistle. Duck and Goose took off toward her. The big horses reared in unison and kicked a raider each. The two men collapsed unconscious in the road.

The fourth and final raider looked panicked. He threw down his weapons and hit his knees, begging.

Mags divested him of his weapons. "If Ulf finds out you gave up like this, he'll slit your throat."

The man nodded. "I know. Please . . ."

"If he finds out you said please, he'll bring you back to life and slit your throat again," Mags said.

"We were to delay you. Hold you until he catches up."

"Why?" Ava asked. "We're doing what he wants."

"You're doing what Angmere wants," the man said.

"And Ulf has a different agenda," Ava said. She looked at Mags for confirmation.

"I don't think Ulf wants us to succeed. I think he wants to take our bounty for himself," Mags said.

"What are we gonna do?" Eldon asked. "Wait for him and kill him?"

"No. That won't help us. It'll just delay us and he wants that. Besides, we won't be able to kill him, not out here. He won't come alone and he won't give up so easy as old boy here." Mags motioned to the Norrikmen.

"How are we going to deal with him then?" Dane asked. He gathered up Duck and Goose and soothed them.

"We're going to leave his toys for him right here and we're going to hurry up and find those women before he does." Mags dug in her bags and handed everyone some leather ties. "Truss them all up nice and tight. Oh and take their clothes. Just for good measure."

"Don't do this. He'll kill us," the talkative Norrikman pleaded.

"You're right," Mags said. She pulled her batons and broke his arms. "There. You're fine now."

As the Trio tied the Norriks, Mags pretended to fix Duck's tack as she contemplated her strategy. Ulf would have to be dealt with. She really needed to find the women before Ulf did and not just for her own and the Trio's preservation. Mags feared for the women if he found them first. She knew she had a head start on him, but that wouldn't last. She had to move faster and find the trail. Many lives depended on it.

CHAPTER

NINETEEN

The remainder of the travel to Sheaf was uneventful. They made good time, covering more miles per day than Mag's would have bet on with three people on foot. The Trio may have been green at the criminal business, but they were young, strong, and clearly used to travel.

Dane was tall, so his long stride ate up the miles. Ava was small, but the girl seemed never to tire. She was the first one awake every morning and the last one asleep at night. Even Eldon kept pace, proving his legs were as strong as his mouth. Neither ever seemed to stop. He complained non-stop about his lack of a horse. Mags wouldn't let him steal any horses from Calen and she had gifted Ance's poor white horse to the needy family. Eldon was horrified by the gift and didn't understand why he couldn't have the white horse.

"Because you haven't earned an animal yet," Mags said.

"I have enough money for a horse," Eldon replied. He kicked a few rocks in the road in frustration.

Duck and Goose both snorted at him and eyed him. Mags patted Duck.

"Anyone can buy an animal. Earn one instead," Mags countered.

"I have no idea what you're talking about," Eldon scoffed. From the look on his face, Mags knew he thought she was crazy.

Dane walked up beside Goose. He cut up a piece of apple and gave it to the big horse. Goose nickered at him and took the slice, crunching it contentedly. He gave Duck a slice as well. Mags smiled at the exchange, then looked at Eldon.

"If you're confused, ask your buddy. He gets it."

When they reached Sheaf, they made camp on the Mirrik side of the river. Mags left the Trio with the horses at camp, then ferried to the other side of the river and took Ance into Sheaf. She had been right; Ance was worth something in Sheaf. She turned him in to the local law and received twenty copper. Ance was indeed a cutthroat and was wanted for some nasty stabbings.

After collecting the bounty, Mags took a walk around Sheaf, inquiring at the docks about the two women and making good use of the money to ensure the captains and riverboat men told her the truth.

Nobody had seen the two women. If they hadn't gone to Sheaf, then maybe they'd crossed the river further south. Or maybe they had taken a barge all the way down to the sea. They could have skirted Sheaf and gone overland to Watchpoint. There were many possibilities and she had very little to go on, other than the vague descriptions and the knowledge that they were only a couple of days ahead of her. She and the Trio had made such good time from Calen that unless the two women had taken a boat down the river, an expensive option, she had to be close to catching up. But she was uncertain. Had it been a regular bounty, Mags would have to make her best guess and move fast. But it was not a regular bounty and she did have an option.

That option weighed heavy on her heart and mind. It was

dangerous; however, the trail had gone cold and there were simply too many possibilities of routes and too little time for her to narrow them down in any conventional way.

Mags ferried back across the river and grabbed some rope from her pack. She turned to the Trio.

"I'm going to need you to tie me up, then leave me. Keep moving down river. I'll catch up." She handed the rope to Dane. "Tie it tightly to my wrist, then around that big tree, then to my other wrist."

"Are you nuts?" Ava asked.

"Do it and don't delay. Get moving," Mags said.

Dane nodded and tied her.

"Take Duck and Goose. I'll find you."

"Seriously? We're just going to do this? What are you going to do?" Ava yelled.

Dane grabbed her arm, and Ava yanked it away.

"I'm not leaving until I get an explanation," Ava said.

"I'm going to call an old friend. Stay away. Don't come near me and when he comes, don't go near him." Mags pulled at the ropes. They were tight and strong, but would they be strong enough? She didn't know and uncertainty in this situation, with the Trio refusing to leave, made her hesitate. But only for a second. She was out of time and she needed his help.

Under the ancient oak, Mags closed her eyes and focused on the sounds of the forest. She let the chirping of the birds and the scurrying of the little creatures relax her. When she felt calm and centered, she turned her arm over. She concentrated on a specific creature, not one of the normal animals of the forest, and then she listened to her own heartbeat. After a few minutes, she began to hear a second heartbeat. Its beat was slightly out of rhythm. Faintly at first but then louder and louder until its volume and its beat matched hers and the two sounds melded into one. The place where Matchi marked her began to burn and glowed blue.

The great hound stepped out of the underbrush. His hackles were raised and he growled. His nostrils flared and he sniffed the air. He seemed to recognize the scent and he advanced on Mags. He got within a few inches of her face, then he stuck out his huge tongue and licked the entire side of her face. She opened her eyes, smiled, and petted him as best she could, tied up as she was. "Hello, old friend."

He whined and nudged her with his big head, then laid down beside her and rolled against her, nearly shoving her over as he attempted to crawl into her lap. She laughed.

"I know, I know. It's been a while." She scratched him behind his ears. He squealed contentedly. "I need your help." Mags held out her arm. The hound sniffed the spot. He looked up at her and his eyes glowed red. Mags felt her eyes get hot, and as she stared into the hound's eyes, her own vision became red-tinged. She panted along with him and their heartbeats merged again. Mags closed her eyes and she could see the two women. They didn't skirt Sheaf. They didn't head overland toward Watchpoint. They didn't take a boat downriver. Mags saw them following the river on the Mirrik side all the way down to the narrow point that forded the Arlean.

The hound howled, long and sorrowful, then he growled, the deep notes of it rumbled and shook everything around them. Mags did the same and soon they were growling and panting together. The big beast snarled and drool dripped from his lips as he stamped his feet, eager to run. He took off into the forest.

Mags thrashed and pulled at the ropes. She foamed at the mouth and soon the whole of her shirtfront was soaked with it. All she could think about was quarry, running something down and devouring it.

Somewhere in her peripheral vision, a red blob appeared. She understood that she should recognize it but she didn't. She only knew it was big and its heart beat in its chest. Then a smaller red form appeared, then a third. All three of the hearts were visible to her. They glowed red inside the blobs and when they all beat faster and more irregular Mags sniffed the air and smelled the intoxicating scent of fear.

She snarled and yanked at the ropes. The knots at her wrists strained at the force, and the extra flex she got when she pulled encouraged her to pull harder. She did and kept doing it, and when she let out a nasty foaming growl of rage, the rope finally snapped. Mags lunged toward the nearest red blob. She knocked it down and pounced on its chest. The bright red heart in the thing beat so fast it sounded like one continuous thing. Mags was just about to rip that heart out of the thing and devour it when something grabbed her from behind.

Great arms like iron bands wrapped around her, holding her in place even as she thrashed with all her strength. Familiar yet unnamable voices yelled, clearly panicked. Mags stretched her neck down and bit one of the big arms holding her. She bit deep and shook her head. The big thing screamed in pain but it held tight. She let go and was about to bite the other arm when one of the smaller red blobs in front appeared. It held something over its head and before Mags could do anything else, the small red blob swung the object at her head. It connected with a solid thwack, then everything went black.

WHEN MAGS OPENED HER EYES, her vision was back to normal and the hound was gone. That didn't matter. Nobody but her could see him anyway, making any explanation even more difficult. She was trussed up like a hog waiting for the spit. The Trio stood watch around her. They kept their distance and fear resided in their eyes.

"It's okay. It's me again. I won't hurt you," Mags said.

"What the hell was all that?" Ava asked. "You went insane and nearly killed us."

"Yes. That's what happens. Look, I'm sorry. I did warn you though."

"You could have warned us you'd try and eat Ava," Eldon said. He stayed back farthest. Dane was closest and he looked afraid, but also worried about her. He held his arm where she'd bitten him.

"I said I was sorry, okay? Now untie me. We don't have much time."

"No way. She'll kill us," Eldon said. He crossed his arms and shook his head.

Ava also hesitated. She was afraid but didn't want to seem like she was afraid, so she stood closer and looked as though she wanted to untie Mags, but she didn't.

Dane untied her. "I don't know what that was, but I know you. You've had plenty of chances to kill us or leave us and you didn't."

Mags stood up and rubbed her sore wrists. The ropes had cut deep and the burns stung, but they were healing. "Thanks." She held out her arm. The mark still glowed blue, and it burned when she started north. When she turned south, the burning stopped. If Mags went in the wrong direction, it would always burn.

"I know where they're going. If we go now and move fast, we should be able to get ahead of them.

CHAPTER
TWENTY

How are we going to get ahead of them when they're two days ahead of us and we're on foot?" Ava asked as they broke camp as quickly as possible.

"We're going to take a shortcut," Mags answered. "They're going to Arlea. They'll cross at Narrowspont. We're going to catch a barge, take it downriver, and beat them to The Arlean."

"I thought they were going to Kos," Dane said. He packed up in his usual efficient manner and was ready to move before anyone.

Mags mounted Duck and nodded. "They'll head to Arleasport. It's a big place. They'll have no trouble catching a ship to Kos."

"So then how are we going to get them?" Ava asked. Since the attack, the girl had kept her distance but tried to look like she wasn't afraid.

"We're going to get to Arleasport first and we're going to watch the docks." Mags squeezed Duck forward, and Goose followed.

"They could go lots of ways. I don't think we should just bet on them going to Arlea."

"I'm not betting. I know," Mags said. She and Duck moved into a fast walk and Goose followed. She heard the Trio scramble to keep up. The pace set forced Ava and Eldon into a jog, but Dane kept up with his same, steady walk. It wasn't long before he pulled even with Goose, who whinnied at him.

"What are we going to do when we catch them?" Dane asked.

"Take them back," Mags said. She scowled thinking about it. The women had to go back either way. Better with her than with Ulf.

"I don't know what they did, but I know Angmere. Whatever it was, it won't be cause enough for whatever punishment he has in mind for them. I don't think we should take them back," Dane said.

"I have no choice," Mags replied, perhaps a bit grumpier than she meant it to sound. She didn't know Angmere, not the way the Trio did, but she agreed that whatever he had in mind for this quarry wouldn't be just. She didn't want to return the women. Even as she thought it, the blue mark on her skin burned. Mags grimaced and rubbed it. Worse would come if she refused Matchi's order.

"We always have a choice," Dane said. He quickened his pace just a bit and Goose followed him.

Mags soured even more. She put Duck into a trot. They passed Dane and Goose. Goose broke into a trot beside her. Nobody said anything until they came to a barge loading spot along the river.

There were three docks. Some laden with merchandise and dry goods, some with produce and animals, and some with passengers waiting to board. Mags smiled when she recognized an old friend.

Mags had known Orin since he had been a baby-faced deckhand. Now a grizzled, seasoned pilot of the Trades, he owned his own boat. She dismounted and led Duck over to the captain. When he saw her, he grinned and went to clasp her arm.

"I'd heard you were in the North. Working I suppose," Orin said.

"Always," Mags replied. "I need to get to Arleasport. Fast."

"Just you?" Orin asked.

"No. Me, the boys"—Mags pointed to the horses—"and them."

Orin looked to the Trio, who had just caught up, red-faced and panting from the pace. Ava scowled. Eldon bent over as he caught his breath. Dane didn't complain.

"This is a first," Orin said. "But then you've always had a soft spot for strays, even if you're loathe to admit it."

Mags rolled her eyes at him as he laughed. "You have space available?"

"For you and your little pack? Always," Orin said. He pointed to a neat, white barge minimally loaded with a few goats and chickens. "That one's going south within the hour. You'll be in Arleasport in three days."

"Excellent!" Mags shook his arm again. She pulled out her coin. "How much?"

"Let's say five."

Mags scowled. "That's not even close to standard."

"No. It's just for the horses. You've always got big ones. They take big shits."

"That's not fair," Mags said. She counted out twenty and held it out to him, but he only took five.

"I still owe you for that trouble up the Brunland."

"That was ages ago. We're taking up paying space," Mags said.

He shrugged. "It's my space. I say how much. Either get on or don't. The bell's in a quarter hour from now. Hopefully those monsters took a shit on the road." He nodded to Duck and Goose, who eyed him and snorted as if offended.

"Alright, but I'll not forget the debt," Mags said. She motioned to the Trio. "We're taking this barge."

Eldon shook his head. "No way. I hate boats. Boats sink. Water. There's things in there. Nope."

"We don't have time to debate. The boat is fast," Mags said. She led Duck and Goose across the gangplank and onto the barge.

"No. I said no and that's what I meant. I'm putting my foot down!" Eldon stomped and crossed his arms. He turned pale and sweaty.

"He fell out of a boat once and he can't swim," Ava said. She didn't hesitate. She got on the boat and sat down on some bundles of hay.

"Well then, don't fall out. You'll be fine." Mags came back across the plank.

"No. I-I'll go overland and meet you there. Give me some coin. I'll buy a horse." Eldon shook his head and refused to move.

"That won't be faster, and I've told you several times, I'm not buying you a horse," Mags said. "Let's go. Move."

"Look, you're not the boss of me. I say when I move and where I go and I say there's no way—"

Mags swept his feet out from under him. She put a knee on his back, then pulled some cord from her belt. She hog-tied him then nodded at Dane.

Dane picked him up and carried him aboard. Eldon kicked and screamed.

"Dane, you Son-of-a-goat-sucking, You better put me down and untie me or I swear on Oldam's Left Nut I will—"

As Dane deposited Eldon gently into a bed of straw on the deck, his sister gagged him. He cursed her through the fabric. She glared at him and he at least stopped the violent thrashing, though he mumbled low obscenities at her.

Mags somehow held back laughter.

Ava looked at her and shrugged. "We gag him a lot."

"We'll all enjoy the peace." Mags boarded and sat down on the hay bale. It was a medium sized barge with a wide, flat deck, meant for moving stock and produce up and down the river. There was room for the occasional passenger, but this trip, there were only a handful. It relaxed her a bit.

But just as she relaxed, three men boarded. Mags kept her smile even as she recognized them from the camp outside of Calen. They tried to act casual and avoid eye-contact. That told her everything she needed to know.

CHAPTER
TWENTY-ONE

The barge departed on time. It pushed away from the dock and was soon underway, riding the swift current and making excellent time south. After a bit, Eldon quieted. Dane removed the gag and untied him. He glared at his sister and Mags but didn't say anything.

The sun dipped low on the horizon and the late afternoon light shimmered and glowed against the calm surface of the river. Mags relaxed against the side of the boat. There were five other passengers, including the three men from Calen. The other two were plain travelers, not mercs at all. The mercs from Calen tried to mimic them, but Mags had always found mercenaries and cutthroats to have a way about them that couldn't be masked. They were twitchy and planning for a fight even as they pretended they were not. The one who had watched her in the camp kept glancing over at her. Mags debated the play. She didn't really want to fight on the deck. There wasn't much room and even though the waters were calm and the deck flat, it wasn't a stable surface, especially not if the fight started a great commotion.

The only merc that mattered was the rat-faced one. Mags

wanted to know who had hired them. She could get that information from him. The other two were just in the way. It would be four on three, advantage to her, except Ava was too small to do what was required, although Mags had no doubt the girl would enjoy it. Though they'd untied Eldon, he was too motion sick to help. The man for the job was Dane. He was twice as big as either of the two men. The problem was, Dane didn't have an aggressive bone in his body. Still, he was the best option.

Dane stood next to the horses. The big kid stroked them as he watched the sun set. Mags eased over and ran her hands over Duck's foreleg as if examining him. Dane immediately bent down, a look of concern on his face.

"Is he okay?"

Mags kept her voice low and even but didn't whisper. "He's fine. When I say go, I want you to walk over to those two guys hanging out by the bags of grain and chuck them both overboard."

Dane looked confused and horrified. "Why would I do that? They're not bothering us."

Mags didn't reply. She just stared at him a second or two and to his credit, the big guy understood. He nodded and stood up.

Mags turned and stretched. She twisted her head and cracked her neck, then she yawned. "Go," she said.

For a big kid, Dane was fairly quick. Big guys were most generally slow and awkward. Dane was just sort of awkward sometimes. But in this case, he moved efficiently and in two quick, smooth motions, grabbed both of the mercs and tossed them into the river. Before the rat-faced one could react, Mags grabbed him and tossed him to the deck. She slammed herself onto his back and pinned him down. He struggled but Mags mashed the side of his face into the decking.

"You can tell me who hired you or join your friends in the drink. Choose wisely. That water is cold," Mags said.

"You're a crazy bitch! Captain! Captain! Get her off me!" The

115

deckhands and the captain ignored him. The man bucked and tried to dislodge her with a practiced wrestling flip to gain position, but Mags was ready for him. She slammed her knee directly into his crotch and held it there, then twisted his wrist and arm upward, straining it until she heard it creak in the socket. He screamed.

"Who hired you?" Mags asked again. She cracked his nuts with her knee again. "If I have to ask a third time, you lose them."

Ava pulled out her dagger and bent down, smiling at the man. "Let me do it."

"A woman. Big one. She paid me to jump anyone who came through asking about her!" the man yelled. "Come on, let me up."

"That was clever of her," Mags said. "Pickings must be slim in the merc department though." She let him go. "Now you're going to sit quietly way over there until we get to the port."

He rubbed his arm and winced at his bruised balls, then glowered at Mags. He got to his feet, then quick as lightning, pulled two daggers and shoved them into Mag's chest.

The force of it knocked her onto her back. Mags lay on the deck as her chest burned. She stared up at the twilight sky and closed her eyes for a moment, then she opened them and stood up.

"I'll kill you for that!" Ava screamed and threw herself at him. Her daggers flashed and the merc smirked at her as he sidestepped her angry attack. He grabbed her by the scruff and threw her overboard.

Dane clobbered the merc and sent him flying.

"She can't swim either!" Eldon yelled. He went to the side of the boat and seemed like he was going over, but he paled and could only grip the rail with white knuckles.

Mags pulled the knives from her chest and threw them to the

deck. She ran to the side and dove into the water. Ava struggled to float and her panicked flailing ensured her failure. Mags swam to her and grabbed her. The floundering, terrified girl groped for her, then disappeared beneath the surface of the water. Mags reached down and grabbed her again. Ava spat out a mouthful of water and looked to Mags. In that moment, Mags saw a scared kid, not an angry one. Ava had dropped the mask.

"Calm down. I got you. Just relax," Mags said as she got an arm around Ava's waist. Ava latched onto her neck and the force dunked them both. Mags kicked up and they surfaced. "You have to calm down or we'll both drown. You'll float. Just kick your legs, back and forth." Mags held them both there, treading water and soon, Ava calmed down and kicked, mimicking Mags. "That's it. Good. We gotta get back to the boat."

"Don't let go of me," Ava said. Her hand grabbed at Mag's clothes.

"I won't, I promise. Let your body float, onto your stomach, like this." Mags kicked up and shifted weight so they we both on their stomachs. "Good, okay, now just kick easy."

They both kicked and began moving faster toward the boat. The current helped. "See, it's easy. Kick a little harder."

Ava was still jerky and afraid, but she was getting better and calmer. Mags kicked harder and soon they were within pole range of the boat. The captain held out the pole and Mags guided Ava to it. They pulled the girl close and Dane reached over the side and pulled her from the water. Mags swam closer and before she could grab the side of the boat, Dane hauled her on the deck.

Everyone stared at her. She had two huge rips in her shirt where the knives had gone into her chest, and the fabric was pink as the blood washed out in the swim. "That's like the third shirt this week," Mags said.

She stalked over to the merc. He was groggy, but conscious.

Mags pulled a cord and bound the man's hands. She yanked the knot extra-tight and he squawked, opening his eyes and blinking them. When he focused on her, they grew wider, and she read recognition and fear in them.

"You should be dead. I got you right in the—"

She didn't let him finish. Mags picked him up and threw him into the river. He floundered and yelped as he bobbed and disappeared beneath the surface.

"I thought you didn't kill people?" Ava asked. She huddled under a blanket and scooted closer to Dane, who was always warm.

"I didn't kill him," Mags said. She went to her bags and pulled out dry clothes, including her last whole shirt.

"You tied him up and chucked him in the river," Ava said.

"No worse than he did to you." Mags used the horses for cover and changed clothes. She stayed next to them and let their body heat warm her.

"What if he doesn't know how to swim?" Eldon asked. He sat on the other side of Ava, almost protectively.

"There's no time like the present to learn," Mags said.

She leaned into Duck and rubbed her chest to move the warmth through her. It was tender where the knives had stuck, but nearly completely healed. Everyone on the boat had seen them stick, had seen the blood bloom. They all kept their distance and stared at her. Mags saw the familiar look of fear in their eyes. Except for Ava's. Ava looked at her with curiosity and a slight, grudging respect. Somehow, Mags found that more unnerving than the fear. For once, she was the one to look away.

She settled in next to the horses and turned her attention to the bow and the direction of travel. There was danger behind, with Ulf's pursuit. There was danger ahead, with the women clearly not being scared, running prey. Those things further complicated an already complicated and difficult task. But in that moment, Mags chose not to focus on that. At the moment, everyone was safe. She had plenty of information, and if the current held its good speed, they would beat everyone to Arelasport and there, Mags had help. That gave her a glimmer of hope and as that little spark kindled, the Voice returned, humming that old lullaby. It seemed meant to comfort Mags.

She surprised herself and let it.

CHAPTER

TWENTY-TWO

As promised, the barge docked in Arleasport early in the morning of the third day. They gathered their gear and the horses, disembarking before the deckhands began unloading the cargo and livestock. Mags shook hands with the captain and gave him a few extra coins, which he tried to refuse.

"Orin wouldn't like it," the captain said.

Mags made him take it. "I didn't count on all that disturbance. Just take it. What Orin doesn't know won't hurt him. And do me a favor. Keep it quiet we were onboard."

He nodded and took the coin, then went back to his duties.

The port was busy for so early in the day, but that was normal in the big places of the world. Business never slept. Dockers loaded and unloaded every kind of good imaginable— produce, livestock, weapons, lumber, skins, leather, grain— anything and everything.

While the commercial docks were busy, the passenger queues were empty. The ships would sail for Kos and other ports on the Beacon Sea with the tide, which wasn't favorable

until later in the day. That was perfect. It would give them time
to set the trap.

"Where are we going?" Ava asked. "Shouldn't we wait here
and make sure they don't get past us?"

"You can if you like. I'm going to go find some breakfast,"
Mags said. "They won't get past us. They're behind us." She
started down the waterfront. Eldon and Dane followed. Ava
scowled, then followed too.

Mags led them to a tavern with an attached livery. A young
stableboy greeted them.

"Best livery in Arleasport. We'll groom and feed 'em. The
good grain, not that Rousland stuff with sawdust you get north
of here."

The Trio bristled. Mags patted the boy on the back. "You
don't need to sell me." She handed him a few coins.

He bowed and went to take the horses but looked confused
and a little frightened when they wouldn't move.

"I'll take them," Dane said. He started into the stable and
Duck and Goose followed him.

According to the sign on the front, the name of the tavern
was The Battered Cod. A picture of a bashed fish with two x's for
eyes decorated the sign. Mags knew it well. She'd used the place
as a sort of base when in the west for many years. She'd seen it
through four owners, the most recent of which was a brother and
sister named Eddie and Jane. When Mags entered, Eddie was
behind the bar. His curly red hair had thinned, and he sported a
patchy red beard. He'd gotten heavier since she'd seen him last,
which was something because he had always been on the big
side. He had also always been on the surly side and that side
tended to be accentuated when Mags was around. This time was
no different. When he saw her, Eddie rolled his eyes and huffed.

"Not you again," he said.

Mags sat down at the bar. A fat black cat jumped up on the

stool next to her. She stroked him. "Hello, Cheese. You're looking well." The cat purred. Mags looked to Eddie. "Oh, Eddie. You're still here."

"Find another tavern, Magdalena. We're full." Eddie wiped down the bar and glared at her.

The tavern was completely empty. "It doesn't look like you're full up," Mags said. She picked up the cat and cuddled him.

"Well, we are," Eddie grumbled.

"Look what we have here!" A woman's voice boomed from the second-floor walkway that led to the rooms of the tavern. A short woman with lots of curly red hair grinned down at them.

Mags stood up from the barstool and grinned back. "Janie."

The woman's eyes twinkled. She ran down the stairs and threw herself into Mags's arms. Mags caught her and hugged her tightly. The woman pulled back from the embrace, smiled at Mags for a beat, then she grabbed Mags's face and kissed her full on the lips. When the kiss ended, Mags was a little dazed. She glanced over at the Trio and they stared at the two women as if they had suddenly sprouted horns and wings. Mags turned her attention back to Jane.

"I guess you missed me," she said.

"I didn't," Eddie said.

"Shut up, Edward," Jane said. "Nobody was talking to you."

"Janie, I can't stay. I just wanted to say hello. Eddie here tells me that you're full up. I'll just head on down to The Crab Pot and get a room there." Mags looked over at Eddie and gave him a sly grin as she waited for the explosion from Jane.

"Full up? We're not even close!" Jane disentangled herself from Mags, walked over to her brother, and slapped him hard. "We have plenty of rooms and we'll always have room for you. Who are your little friends?" She motioned to the Trio, then eyed Dane and smirked.

"They're working with me. Dane, Ava, and Eldon." Mags

could barely say "working with." The words seemed to catch in her throat and make it itch as she avoided Jane's eyes.

"I'm sorry, they're doing what?" Jane asked. She widened her eyes and acted overly surprised.

Mags rolled her eyes at the sarcasm. "I said what I said."

"Hey, I think it's cute. You, a mommy, after all these years." Jane giggled, then hugged Mags and pressed herself against her. "Well, welcome, little ducks. I'm Jane, the owner and boss of this establishment." She looked over at Eddie and scowled. "That's my brother, Edward. He is also here." Eddie flipped her a rude hand gesture which Jane returned. She then ignored him as he slammed around the bar. She smiled at the Trio. "Have you eaten? Sit down. I'll bring breakfast out."

They relaxed at one of the tables. Jane brought out hot food and everyone dug in. She pulled up a chair next to Mags.

"You look good, Maggie."

"You look pretty fine yourself," Mags said. She ate her fill and leaned back in the chair, sipping a hot tea as she admired her friend.

"Of course I do," Jane laughed. She scrunched up her curly hair and shook it out. "I assume you're working."

"Good assumption," Mags said. "Can you get word to Spiro? I need some eyes."

"Of course. Gate or Docks?"

"Both."

Jane whistled but before she could ask, Mags dropped a bag of coins on the table. "As many as he has."

"I've never seen you go all out for normal work. Is this—"

Mags nodded. "Unfortunately."

Jane's face reddened and she huffed. "As if she hasn't already taken enough from you."

"Easy, Janie. That kind of talk only makes it worse," Mags said. She patted Jane's hand.

"I don't give a fiddler's fart about her. She doesn't listen and she'd never deign come this far north anyway." Jane spat on the floor in disgust. "Useless."

"She listens when she wants to and believe me, this one is interesting to her," Mags said.

"What is she talking about?" Ava said.

"Her boss, Matchi, the Huntress," Jane said. "They don't know?"

Mags shook her head. "They were out for it."

"But they've seen you get stabbed and such?"

"Several times now."

Jane looked at the Trio. "Did you guys think that was normal?"

"Of course we didn't," Ava snapped. "Do we look stupid?"

Jane looked at Eldon, then at the other two. "Not all of you. But you do look like young and inexperienced Rouslanders."

"You got a problem with Rouslanders?" Ava bristled.

"I don't have a problem with anyone, except Eddie," Jane said. She didn't back down from Ava at all. "Unless they start trouble in my place. Are you going to start trouble in my place, young Rouslander?"

Ava stood up and fumed. "Maybe—"

"Ava, sit down." Mags glared at the girl. "Janie?" She raised an eyebrow at her friend.

"No, I don't think you'll start much trouble." Jane smiled. "So what do you little ducks know about Matchi, the Huntress?"

"Not much," Dane said. He put a hand on Ava's arm and the girl calmed and sat down. "She's not big where we're from."

"Don't let her hear you say that," Mags said.

"She makes life difficult for Maggie," Jane said. "She must want the quarry you're after because Maggie wouldn't go to this much expense for just any bounty."

"What do you mean?" Ava asked. "A Norrik warlord idiot wants this bounty. He's the one paying."

Jane grabbed Mags's arm and turned it over. The blue mark

was there, faint now, but still there. "That's Matchi's mark. When Mags has it, it's Matchi's."

"Janie, don't. They don't need—" Mags growled.

"The hell they don't. They need to understand what's going to happen if you don't deliver." She pointed at the Trio. "If Mags doesn't catch and deliver this bounty, she won't just lose money. Matchi will have her tormented."

"What does she care? She doesn't die. I've seen her skewered three times now. She's fine," Eldon said.

"That's not what tormented means. Death would be preferable," Jane said. "If Mags doesn't do what Matchi wants, Matchi will call in her little friend, Torment. Torment will do what he does best, which is make Mags suffer. Pain and terribleness you can't even imagine."

"And you can? Has he done it to you?" Ava snarked.

Jane looked over at Mags and cocked an eyebrow. "You're traveling with her? Really?" Mags shrugged and Jane continued, "No, he has not. But I was there once when he did it to Maggie. If you had seen it, you wouldn't have all that attitude, little duckling Rouslander, and you wouldn't ever want to see anyone go through it ever again."

"Easy, Janie." Mags reached out and took Jane's hand and held it. "It will be fine. I know where they're headed. If Spiro can keep his eyes on them, it will all turn out fine."

"Who stabbed you recently?" Jane asked.

"Pitiful excuse for a merc. They hired him to bushwhack us," Mags said. She patted her chest. "No big deal."

Jane rolled her eyes. "You wouldn't say that if you'd ever seen you stabbed. It stops my heart every time."

Mags ran a hand through Jane's red curls. "Your heart?" She winked at her.

"My heart. Yours keeps beating," Jane said. She plopped herself in Mag's lap and kissed her. "Thankfully."

"How did they know to jump us? We were behind them. They couldn't have made us, the women, I mean," Dane asked.

"They took a chance. Hired the mercs to watch Calen. They just figured Angmere would send someone after them. It was a smart move," Mags said.

"You admire them?" Ava asked. "They're quarry."

"They're people," Mags said. "And just like you, they're doing what they have to do to survive. If I knew someone would follow me, I would have laid the same trap. Oh, that reminds me. Tell Spiro to keep an eye out for a big, ugly Norrik shit too. He'll know him when he sees him."

"Never in our years together have I ever known one of your visits to be calm and recreational." Jane shook her head, kissed the top of Mag's head, and stood up. "I'm going to go find Spiro. Edward will get you anything you want. On the house."

"No, I won't," Eddie said. He slammed a glass down on the bar.

Everyone ignored him.

CHAPTER
TWENTY-THREE

ags and the Trio stood in the narrow side street that led away from the docks called Pirate's Alley. A dangerous place, smelling of piss, blood, and ale, it was usually inhabited by unsavory characters, pickpockets, and cutthroats. It was the perfect place to observe the docks without being made. Spiro had reported that the women had entered the city but hadn't been seen since. The next step was to watch all the camps, taverns, and of course, the passenger docks.

"Your friend is watching? How do we know?" Ava asked. She eyed everyone and scowled at them.

Mags had a cloak on to disguise herself. The red mark on her cheek and her blue hand were too noticeable, especially in Pirates Alley, where she had collared many bounties. "You won't know he is, that's why he's the best," she said. She poked Eldon. "You could be good at that too if you keep quiet. You're non-descript and you blend. Not with your mouth, though."

"I—" Eldon started to retort, but Dane elbowed him.

"It was a compliment, Eldon. Sort of," Dane said.

"Alright, let's go. Dane's too big to hide and I'll get made sooner or later, so let's let Spiro do his thing. He'll send word when he finds them," Mags said.

"I-I want to stay," Eldon said. "And practice. I won't screw up. I promise."

Mags looked at him for a second. He didn't say the words with any of his normal cheek or boast. She gave him a little smile and nod. "Meet us back at the tavern in an hour."

Mags, Dane, and Ava started back for the tavern, weaving their way through the dark denizens of the alley. When they reached the end and turned out onto a wider street, three mercenaries blocked their path. The men drew their swords. A big woman stepped out from behind them.

The description of her had been true but failed to convey scale. The woman wasn't just big, she was huge. At least six-and-a-half foot, she was the tallest woman Mags had seen in her three hundred years. Her close-cropped blonde hair framed her big face, which was oddly feminine and delicate-looking for someone so large. An ugly scar ran down the left side of her face. One of her ears was cut in half and her left nostril was notched. Mags could tell life with the Norrikmen had been cruel to her. She was armored with boiled leather and she wielded her short sword like somebody who knew how, grasping it gently as she relaxed.

"I hear you're looking for me," she said. Her voice was deep and raspy, much like Angmere's sorceress's voice.

"It's very kind of you to come find me," Mags said, keeping her tone polite. The mercs were pros too, not like the rat-faced man on the ship, but competent. Mags could tell from the condition of their weapons and the fact that they didn't smell like a barn. This would not be an easy fight.

"I know Angmere hired you. I'm telling you right now, give it up. The money isn't worth it," the big woman said.

"Money seldom is," Mags said. "Look, before you start something unwise, let's talk. My name is Magda—"

"I know who you are." She pointed to Mag's blue hand. "And what you are. I know if you were here for that, we wouldn't be talking. So if you can see reason, just let the bounty go. You don't know Ulf and that witch. They won't pay you anyway."

"Angmere will pay us," Ava growled. She pulled her daggers and her eyes flashed as she glanced between the mercs.

Mags could feel the anger and energy rolling off Ava. Her stomach did a little flip. That would make matters much worse.

The big woman scoffed at Ava. "Child, you know nothing about Annik politics. Angmere is a joke. Ulf and the witch are in charge."

"It doesn't matter. We got hired to take you down. It makes no difference to us who pays or what they do with you," Ava said.

"It doesn't?" The big woman ignored Ava and looked to Mags. "That's not what I hear about you. At any rate, leave us alone, and your pets keep their lives."

"We're not pets and you're talking too much," Ava spat. She threw one of her daggers and hit one of the mercs in the shoulder, then launched herself at him.

Dane looked horrified and stunned at the same time, and when one of the mercs attacked him, he froze.

Mags pulled her batons and stepped in front of Dane, blocking the merc's sword. She disarmed him. "Ava, stand down!" she yelled, blocking the thrust of the second merc. Ava ignored her. "Dane! Grab her before she—"

Mags had to turn her attention back to her own fight as the big woman joined the merc in attacking her. She disarmed the man and cracked him in the knees with her batons. The big woman held back a moment and Mags saw a flash of panic roll across her face.

Dane grabbed for Ava, but in her rage, she slashed at him, opening up a deep wound on his arm. Dane screamed and Ava snapped out of it. She dropped her dagger and turned to him.

"Dane? I'm-I'm sorry. I-I—"

The merc Ava had been fighting regrouped and was poised to take out both Dane and Ava. Mags saw it all and knew she couldn't get there fast enough to stop it, even though time had slowed to that unpleasant, prickling crawl that only happened when you were helpless to stop the terrible thing about to happen.

But the terrible thing didn't happen. The merc stopped his attack and stared at Mags. In fact, all three mercs did. They not only stopped, but they dropped their swords.

Mags's stomach lurched again and the red mark on her cheek began to burn, a sting at first, then like a firebrand had scorched her flesh. She screamed and fell to her knees. Her eyes burned too and her vision blurred, then a red film seemed to wash over it. Her hand itched, then burned, growing hotter as the blue color deepened. Her fingers cracked as the bones broke, then melted into a glowing blue mass. The burning worsened and her hand changed color again, this time to a molten yellow. The mass bubbled and shimmered, then began to lengthen, then curve into a sickle, sharp and deadly. The yellow faded to red, then a dark cobalt blue as the metal hardened. Mags screamed as it did, the pain radiating throughout her entire body.

When she caught the scent of her quarry, the pain stopped and she climbed to her feet. All around her, the people stared. The mercs turned and ran away. The big woman, Dane, and Ava all stared at her with open mouths and terrified expressions on their faces. None of them should have been worried. She wasn't after them. The trail was clearly marked in red for her, but she was the only one who could see it. The red marks glowed and Mags felt a great urge, an indescribable pull at her guts to follow it and hunt.

Many times, when a Harvest came to her, she would run miles and miles. She never tired during it no matter how far the distance. Fortunately, this time, the run was short. Mags ran to the far end of town, a craggy place on the sea. The waves continually crashed against the rocky outcrop, forming the stones into sharp, jagged daggers that would rip bare feet to shreds.

A gaunt young man, not far past eighteen perched on the rocks. He threw a cast net out into the foaming sea. When he pulled it back in, he seemed overjoyed at the tiny baitfish that the cast yielded. He shoved them in his mouth greedily, not caring they were raw. The look on his face was joy at hunger sated, then worry as he frantically readied the net for another cast, hopeful and desperate for more fish.

He didn't see Mags at all, so focused was he on his catch. He had just shoved the last of the minnows in his mouth when Mags's blade sliced through his neck. The look of pleasure at his meager meal was still on his face as his head fell to the crags.

The same feeling of guilt, sadness, shame, and burning pain washed over her. Mags fell to the crags and just like the starving man, she didn't feel them rip her skin. The only pain she felt was the terrible burning as her hand changed back. She rolled over on her back as the burning worsened and her flesh melted. Just as her hand had reverted back to a mess of flesh, the sleep came for her. She dreaded it, that pull toward dreams, the place where she'd have to hear the voices and see the faces of the thousand people she'd taken.

Mags strained her eye muscles and did her best to hold them open, wide, to avoid that sleep, but she wasn't able to avoid it. As her flesh burned and the crags of the shore dug into her back, she drifted off to a terrible nightmare.

CHAPTER
TWENTY-FOUR

I t didn't start how her dreams normally started, with screaming and a rush of faces coming for her, all of them angry, spitting, and snarling. This time when she opened her eyes in the dream, she was staring up at the blue sky. Great tall pines shot up all around her and a pleasant, warm breeze caused the trees to sway gracefully and tickled her face.

When she sat up and looked around, it was familiar. She knew she was in the North, though not as far north as Mirrik or Norrik, so it must have been Rousland. She'd been there before, this exact location. Her cheek burned and she reached up and touched the red spot. Then her hand cramped and when Mags looked down, she saw it was still in the form of the blue sickle.

Mags shook her head no and silently sobbed. She didn't want to do it. She never wanted to do it. She braced herself and waited for the voices, but none came. Instead, someone put a hand on her shoulder and helped her to her feet.

When Mags turned around, a small young woman, quite petite, stood there smiling at her. Mags had seen the woman before. Many times in fact. She had been one of the faces that tormented her after each harvest. But though she knew each one of those faces, she knew this one better than all

132

the rest. *The eyes were familiar. The shape of the nose and the way the woman's lips turned up at the edges were as well-known to her as her own.*

Mags tried to ask, "Who are you?" But in the dream, no voice came from her, she could only mouth the words. The woman didn't answer anyway. She smiled at Mags and took her hand.

She led Mags through the forest to a clearing. A small cabin, well-built and neat, stood in the center. Smoke rose merrily from the chimney and a few fat chickens scratched around in the dirt. There was a small garden, with tender new plants bursting from the good, tilled earth. Sounds of children playing filled her ears. Mags smiled at the sound and turned around to see two blonde children, a little girl and boy, both three or maybe four years old, chasing each other around the clearing. They stopped and waved to Mags and the woman.

Mag's heart stopped when she recognized them. It was Ava and Eldon. The woman waved back to them, then turned and looked at Mags. Her smile faded and her face took on a desperate, pleading look.

"Help them," she said.

Mag's arm acted of its own accord and the sickle slashed through the woman's neck, sending her severed head rolling toward the children. The children screamed and cried. Their screams were joined by the angry voices that Mags knew well. She dropped to her knees and held her hands over her ears, hoping to keep the noise out. It didn't help. She sobbed as the voices cursed her and the two little children screamed for their mother.

CHAPTER
TWENTY-FIVE

When Mags opened her eyes, she realized she wasn't laying on the jagged rocks, but on wet sand, on her back. The waves crashed and rolled and the gulls screamed down at her as she opened her eyes and sat up.

Dane and Ava sat on the sand beside her, a safe distance away. Neither took their eyes off her. Mags quickly assessed the situation. The man's body lay on the crags. Crabs had already come for him. His head was attached. Dane's face read shock and horror, but behind those two things, his caring shone through. Mags knew he had been the one to move her from the rocks. Ava's face read fear and awe—unfortunately, more awe than fear. Ava would have to be abnormal.

Guilt and panic rose in Mags as she looked at Ava and realized what the voice had been trying to tell her. Mags had reaped Ava and Eldon's mother. She swallowed that goiter of guilt down. It was what it was; she couldn't change it. But that didn't make it an easy thing to live with, nor did it make it easy to live with people whose lives she'd ruined.

Mags sighed and flexed her hand. It burned, but it had

returned to human hand shape. As usual it was misshapen and useless, but it would heal. She tested out the rest of her body. She was tired, but fine. "How much did you two see?" she asked.

"All of it," Dane answered. His voice sort of cracked.

"I'm sorry you had to see that. It's not something I want—"

"Are you kidding me? How did you do it? Why can't you do that all of the time? Nobody would stand a chance!" Ava said. Her voice was breathy and excited. "If I could do that—"

"Whoa. Stop right there. First, it's not something I control. Second, if I could control it, I assure you, I would never do it," Mags said.

"Why? It's amazing!" Ava jumped up from the sand and ran to the man. "Why is his head back on? We saw you cut it off, then there was like a flash of light and the next thing we saw was both of you laying on the rocks, but his head was back on."

"Ava, don't ask her that. Can't you see it's painful?" Dane asked.

"Painful? Dane, she's fine. Is this why people can keep killing you and you never die? Can you show me how to do it?" Ava knelt next to her and searched her face. "Please, please show me how to do it."

"I would never wish this on another living soul," Mags said. She stood up and tested her muscles.

"Why? Pain? So what? I can take it. I want it. It made you strong and fast, and you took that guy's head in one swipe, like his neck was made of butter." Ava danced around her. "Show me how."

Mags grabbed Ava and hauled her up so they were nose to nose. "You idiot. You think it's just about pain? The physical pain is nothing. You see that man? He was starving, suffering. I didn't end it, I made it infinitely worse. His soul is gone."

"What? Gone?" Ava asked. "You just killed him. So what?"

"Spoken like someone who has never killed anyone," Mags

spat. She threw Ava to the sand. "I didn't just kill him. I harvested his soul."

"What does that mean?" Dane asked. He helped Ava up from the wet beach.

"I don't know exactly where they go. I only know it's agony. I feel it every time."

"How many times?" Dane asked.

"That was the one thousandth time," Mags said. "I should be done. That was the bargain. Only I'm not. I'm at—never mind. Let's get moving."

Ava exploded. "Oh, right. We're just idiots. You know everything. Oldam's crotch, I'm so sick of it! I'd give anything to have that kind of power, to finally be able to take back what—"

Dane interrupted her. "Ava, calm down, let's just go back—"

"Don't tell me what to do, Dane! You-you . . ."

"I don't know? I do know, Ava. I know everything about you," Dane said. "I've known you your whole life. This thing inside you—you have to give it up."

"Fuck you, Dane. And fuck you, you freak!" Ava screamed. She took off.

"That's an angry kid," Mags said. She watched Ava run, shoving people out of her way as she cut a path of destruction through the docks.

"Yeah. She's . . . Well . . ." Dane shrugged. "She's Ava. I keep hoping we can find a place to-to just live, but she won't and I can't leave her and Eldon."

Mags and Dane started back to the tavern. "They're your family." She paused for a moment. "You all lost your family?"

Dane nodded. "Mine got sick. That was bad enough, but Ava and Eldon? Their mother died when they were three. Their father? Killed by raiders. Ava saw everything. She hates the Norrikmen."

"She's not a killer. None of you are."

"She wants to be or thinks she does. She thinks that will help. Killing them all."

"It won't," Mags said.

"You don't kill with that hate in you. You're not trying to-to change something."

Mags nodded. "That's true. But I've been alive for over three hundred years. I've seen her story before. It only ends in pain."

"You don't need three hundred years to know that," Dane said.

"No. No, you do not." Mags sighed. "The big woman took off?"

"As soon as you, umm, you know." Dane shrugged.

"Yeah. Her mercs ran. Why didn't you follow her?" Mags stumbled as a wave of exhaustion hit her. One of her calves started to cramp and she had difficulty walking. They'd had the woman and now they were back to zero.

Dane grabbed Mags around the waist and supported her as they walked. "Because we were more worried about you."

Mags felt a strange feeling, something she hadn't felt in many years, so distant she didn't really have a name for it anymore, but she knew what it was. It wouldn't last. It couldn't, but just then she was grateful for it and for the big kid helping her walk. She leaned against him. His solid, steady warmth reminded her of her horses. For a second she was frightened by that, but then Dane held her tighter and it calmed her. She smiled up at him. He smiled back. The kid had a way of knowing things and he knew what she felt. He knew what she needed and he gave it.

For once, Mags accepted it.

TWENTY-SIX

When they returned to the tavern, Dane helped Mags sit down in a chair near the fire. Jane brought her a cup of tea and sat down next to her. Her eyes were cloudy and troubled as she stared at Mags.

"How many was that?" Jane asked.

"I don't know," Mags said. She sipped her tea and tried to avoid Jane's gaze.

"You don't know? You, Maggie? Really?"

Mags rolled her eyes. "Janie."

"You added on, didn't you?"

Mags kept quiet. She concentrated on her tea.

Jane grabbed her face and held it. "You were almost done."

Mag's eyes darted toward Dane. Jane followed and sighed. "For him?"

Mags shook her head. "For all of them."

"Magdalena Verran! Three extras?" Jane smacked her, knocking her teacup out of her hand.

"Hey!" Mags scowled at Jane and bent to pick up the cup.

"What's she talking about?" Dane asked.

"Do you know what she is? What she does?" Jane asked him. She brought Mags another cup of tea.

"Jane. Don't." Mags warned.

Jane shook her head. Her face reddened with anger. "No. Shut up, Maggie." She turned back to Dane. "Do you know?"

"Well, I know she's a bounty hunter and umm, I know her hand"—Dane motioned with his own hand, wiggling his fingers —"turns into a sword and she . . . yeah."

"So you don't know. Okay. So when her hand changes she has no choice. One of those—"

"Careful, Janie." Mags warned.

"One of those gods"—Jane spat the word with a hateful tone —"has a job for her to do. She has to do it. And she's been doing it for a very, very long time. She was almost done, the debt nearly paid, but now I learn she's added three harvests."

Dane's face paled and he looked at Mags. "Harvests are lives?"

"Souls. Souls to be collected," Mags said. She sipped her tea.

"So you were nearly square and you added three more souls." Dane looked at Jane.

"Yes. There are three of you, right?" Jane asked him.

Dane nodded. He understood. "That was how you got us out of Angmere's place. You took on more souls. For us. Mags, I don't know what to say."

Mags held up a hand. "There's nothing to say. That's done." She thought of the rest of the bargain and of what she knew now about her part in Ava and Eldon's lives. The guilt washed over her again and she looked at the floor.

Dane put a hand on her knee. "Thank you. That's all I know to say. I owe you my life. We all do. I'll try and make sure Ava and Eldon— "

Mags interrupted him. She couldn't have him making things easy on her. She deserved so much worse and it was she herself who was obligated. "No. It's-it's okay. I'm no innocent, Dane. I deserve everything I've gotten and then some. So don't worry about thanking me or making life easier for me. I don't deserve it."

"That's maybe one of the dumbest things you've ever said," Jane said. She grabbed Mag's chin and tipped it up. She searched Mag's eyes and Jane's sharp skills of observation found out the truth. "This isn't like you. Tell me what else."

Mags looked to Jane, then to Dane. "There are two things. First, we can't fail in this bounty. If it were just Matchi's rage I had to worry about—or Torment—I wouldn't care that much. But there's another part of the bargain. I traded three more Harvests for your lives and that was Kohoc. But Matchi will always have her fun too. She knew I'd likely blow off this bounty once I was clear of Angmere. She added a condition. If those two women are not returned by Midsummer, then the three of you will die."

Dane's breath caught for a second, then he nodded. "Okay, well, I'm okay with—"

"And I'll have to kill you," Mags said.

Dane's face paled and he gulped. "That's not . . . That's . . . yeah. So what's the second thing?"

As Mags was about to tell him about Ava and Eldon's mother, the tavern door opened and Ava stalked in. She sat down on a bench and scowled.

Mags hesitated. The girl was already spoiling for a fight and Mags wasn't sure it was the right time to go picking one. The guilt burned in her guts but she was practiced at managing that. Although knowing the people affected made this much worse, much more awful to manage, she did it anyway. "And there's one more thing—"

"No."

The voice, which Mags now knew to belong to Ava's mother, chose to intervene. Mags listened and stopped. It didn't want her telling Ava, at least not right then. It went against her nature, but the voice had a purpose and Mags thought maybe she should honor its wishes in this, and trust it.

"Nothing, just that I have to add in three more Harvests," she said.

"So what? What's the consequence of adding?" Ava asked.

"Maggie, how long did the previous three take you?" Jane spoke up.

"Well, the last two have been close together, so—"

Jane rolled her eyes. "Maggie."

"A really long time," Mags replied.

Nobody said anything for a bit as Dane and Ava processed the information. Jane smirked. Mags rolled her eyes at that. Jane knew exactly how long the previous three Harvests had taken.

"She added them for us. That's how she got us away from Angmere," Dane said. His voice was quiet and when Mags nodded at him, his eyes grew sad.

"So, what do you want from us? Your choice, not ours," Ava said. The girl crossed her arms and pouted. Defiant was Ava's default when any emotion other than rage came to her.

Jane wasn't amused. She stood up, stalked to Ava and pulled the bench out from under her, sending Ava to the floor. "You ungrateful little shit," she said. "She saved your life."

Ava jumped up and lunged for Jane. Jane punched the girl squarely in the nose. Ava's nose gushed blood, but that didn't stop her. She came for Jane again. Mags laughed and did nothing. She had seen Jane handle grown men three times her size. Jane wasn't in any danger, as Ava was about to find out. Before Ava could learn the consequences of attacking a seasoned tavern proprietor in a seaport, Dane grabbed her.

"Ava. Stop." Ava struggled and kicked at him, but he held her fast. "Stop it. Ow! Quit biting!"

Ava clamped down on his arm and shook it like a dog, but the big guy didn't let go. Mags sighed and got up from her chair. She was sore, but she had mostly healed from the Harvest. She grabbed Ava by the hair and pulled her head back. Dane squeezed Ava tighter, restricting her movement more.

"Knock this shit off right now." Ava winced as Mags pulled harder on her hair. "If you want me to hog tie you, I will. Is that what you want?"

Ava shook her head and sniffed. "Let go of me, Dane." Mags read the rage in the girl's eyes, but it began to fade to normal anger.

Ava nodded to Dane and he released her. The girl sat down on the bench and wiped at her bloody nose. Dane sat beside her, ready to grab her again. Jane threw a towel at the girl. Ava caught it and dabbed at her nose. She stuck out her lip in a pout and glared at Jane, but she made no move.

"Keep it up," Jane growled.

"Janie, please, it's fine," Mags said. She sat down on the bench across from Dane and Ava. She pulled Jane down next to her and kept an arm around the woman. "It's cute when you get all huffy, though." She smiled and kissed Jane on the cheek.

"You're ridiculous too," Jane said. She scowled at Mags. "At this rate you'll never be done," she said. She put a hand on Mags's cheek.

Mags put her hand on top of Jane's. "Of course I will." She winked at Jane. "Are you ready to be rid of me?"

"Never," Jane said. She kissed Mags, then got up. She started for the bar. "I should get to work."

"What happens when she's done?" Dane asked.

Jane stopped and stared at him. "She dies."

Neither Dane nor Ava said anything. They just stared at Mags.

Finally, Ava spoke, but there was no anger in her voice, for once. "Then why would you ever want to be done? You could live forever."

"Ava, we saw it. It hurts," Dane said. He looked at Mags. "It hurts, right?"

Mags nodded. "More every time." She thought about that pain, the agony that compounded over many lifetimes, but that wasn't the worst of it. She looked at Jane and smiled as the affection warmed her heart, but only to a certain point. Mags never let it fully in. There had been many Janes over the years and the pain of watching them grow old or get sick and die dwarfed the physical pain of even a million Harvests.

Ava still didn't understand. "But you heal. I've seen it. You-you could . . ." Mags watched the girl's face and could see the wheels turning in her head as she struggled to see beyond the physical immortality.

Dane, however, understood. His gaze followed Jane as she walked away, and when Mags looked at him, he nodded at her. The big kid had realized the real cost of three more souls. He put a hand on Ava's arm. "Healing isn't always as easy as she makes it look."

"Dane, what are you talking about? She's fine. We've seen—"

Ava stopped when Eldon burst through the door. He struggled to catch his breath, but his eyes sparkled with triumph and excitement.

"I found them!"

TWENTY-SEVEN

W e tracked them! That big woman came busting out of the docks! You can't miss her; she's huge!" Eldon gulped down some water, even as he puffed out his chest, proud of his newfound stealthy prowess.

"Yeah, we know. We saw her too. Almost had her," Ava grumbled.

"But you didn't," Eldon said. He smirked at his sister, unafraid of her anger. "We got her now though. Me and Spiro tracked her to a flophouse. He's got eyes everywhere on it. No way they move without us knowing! We got them!"

"Yeah," Mags said. She knew where the flophouse was, in the less savory part of the town. That didn't concern her. What did was what she was going to do next.

"What are we waiting for?" Ava stood up. "Let's go. I owe that big bit—"

"Sit down," Mags said. "They aren't going anywhere. Think before you act." Ava huffed but sat. Mags tapped the table. "She knows we'll find her. She'll be waiting."

"So we bust in there and take them out fast. No chance for her to do anything," Ava said.

"Ava, she found us first, remember?" Dane said.

"So? That just means she's dumb," Eldon said. He laughed. "Rookie move."

"That woman's no rookie," Mags said. "She didn't want a fight."

"Oh, she didn't? Then why did she hire those guys to jump us?" Ava laughed. "She started it. Now we're gonna finish it!"

"Only people who care about nothing and think they have nothing to lose want a fight," Mags said. "That woman definitely has something to lose. Or someone, rather."

Dane nodded. "The other lady."

"Yes," Mags said. "She didn't want to fight us in the alley and the other woman wasn't there. If she had meant to take us out that way, she could have hired someone to knife us on the sly. She was trying to scare us."

"A bluff? With three mercs?" Ava scoffed. "Dumb. And weak."

"No, not dumb or weak. Reasonable. Smart people avoid sword fights."

"They didn't attack us. We attacked them," Dane said. They both looked at Ava.

"Don't look at me like that, Dane! They had weapons and I-I—"

"Ava, relax. Eldon, run ahead and tell Spiro we're coming." Mags stood up and stretched. Everything was back to normal. The pain was gone and her muscles, while a little tight, felt fine. She cracked her neck. Her hand, however, still wasn't in useable condition. She didn't think that would be an issue, at least not yet. "Let's go and get this over with."

Eldon grinned, then took off. Dane's shoulders slumped and he stood up but wasn't happy. Ava jumped up and checked her daggers.

"You won't need those," Mags said.

Ava rolled her eyes, sighed, then made a show of twirling her daggers and sheathing them with force.

Mags nodded and smirked at Ava, as she patted her on the cheek. "Good. Get it out of your system now." Her last pat was a bit more forceful to Ava's cheek, more slap than pat. Ava's eyes darkened and so did Mags's. They stared at each other for a beat, neither backing down. In Ava's eyes Mags saw a defiance and anger that churned and boiled. She'd seen it before, many times, in the eyes of people she collected and brought to Villeins all over. It was common to the eyes of the Andosh and Darrish alike. And without a doubt, seeing it in a person's eyes was always the harbinger of something dangerous and unpleasant. Luckily, in Ava's eyes she had also seen fear and regret, and at times, love, which told her there was still hope.

Mags gave Ava a little smile, not a smirk, and patted her shoulder. "Stay calm, stay ready. Let's go."

IT DIDN'T TAKE LONG to walk to the flophouse. Mags knew where it was as she had collared several bounties there over the years. She laughed to herself on the walk as she thought about how likely it was she knew the location of every flophouse, tavern, brothel, and general shithole from Gullhome to Abunton. She wasn't sure if that was impressive or depressing.

When they arrived, Eldon was waiting for them in the street in front and her old friend Spiro lurked nearby, hooded and cloaked. When he saw her, he didn't approach. He gave her a nod, then disappeared into the shadows. His business depended on stealth and anonymity. Spiro always assumed someone was watching because he was always watching, so he didn't interact with anyone when he was out and about.

"They're inside!" Eldon was breathless and flushed, clearly excited at his trap.

"Yeah. Good work." Mags gave him a little smile and Eldon beamed.

He puffed up his chest and dusted his knuckles off on his shirt. "It was a nice bit of tailing if I do say so myself."

Mags immediately regretted complimenting him. "Please don't ruin it."

Eldon nodded and stopped boasting. "Yeah. Good call. Umm, so what do we do now?"

Ava grasped her knife handles over and over and Dane fidgeted. They were all nervous.

"Well, first we're going to go inside," Mags said. "Then the three of you are going to stand by the exit. Specifically, Dane. He's big. If they run and get past me, don't let them out."

"What about me and Eldon?" Ava asked.

"You're both with me. But stay back and don't run your mouth," Mags pointed at Eldon, "And don't stab anyone." She pointed at Ava.

"Yeah, Ava, don't stab anyone." Eldon puffed up. His success at tracking and watching had gone to his head.

His sister narrowed her eyes at him, and Eldon gulped and tempered his hubris.

"We need them alive and we need us alive. If I start fighting, you can start fighting. If I don't—"

"Okay, Professor, we got it. Don't do squat until you do squat first. Lesson complete. Can we just do this?" Ava rolled her eyes.

Mags pushed down the urge to punch Ava, but if she were honest, the girl had a point. Not that Mags would ever admit it. She checked her batons even though she didn't expect to need them and walked inside.

It was actually one of the nicer flophouses she had encountered. It approached cleanliness, with floors that appeared to have been swept in the past month and only a dusty, old smell rather than the stank of waste, sweat, and unwashed humans that normally emanated from similar establishments. There were five rooms, three on the ground floor and two on the second level. A flimsy staircase led to a rickety catwalk that connected the two rooms. Mags examined the stairs. They would creak and she doubted they would hold all of their weight. Dane stood in the doorway. His bulk blocked the light from the outside. There were candles scattered about but nobody would waste them in the day, even if a giant blocked the available daylight.

The proprietor of the place, an old man with a long white beard and an eyepatch sat behind a counter. He looked them over, especially Dane. The old man had a wad of chewing tobacco in his mouth. He chewed it vigorously then spat a great mouthful of juice into a horn mug. Mags was impressed he didn't spit on the floor. His gaze moved from Dane to her and Mags saw recognition in his eyes even if she didn't remember him.

"Don't suppose you're wanting a room," he said.

"Not today," Mags replied. "Looking for a big woman."

"This ain't that kind of place. Try two doors down." He spat again in the mug.

"You know that's not what she means, old man," Ava said. She stepped forward and glared at him. The old man eyeballed her. His face didn't change. He looked untroubled as he chewed his wad, like a patient cow. That seemed to upset Ava more.

Mags grabbed her arm and pulled her back. "Relax," she said. She smiled at the old man, pulled a coin from her pocket, and placed it on the counter. "Which room?"

He looked at Ava and chuckled, then he pocketed the coin. "The last one upstairs. You pay for any damages." He pointed at Dane. "And I don't like that big one blocking my light."

"He'll stand inside the door and do his best not to block your light," Mags said.

Dane moved out of the doorway and stood just inside, still

able to cover the door. Mags started up the stairs. The steps creaked and bowed under her weight.

"One at a time on the stairs! You break it, you buy it!" the old man yelled.

Mags held up a hand to Ava and Eldon. "Easy on these. Wait 'til I get to the top."

Mags climbed, placing her feet carefully and avoiding any jolts. Every step was spongy, and she felt like her foot would crash through the wood each time she set it down. The catwalk above wasn't much better, but it was a bit newer wood and felt solid enough although Mags thought they might be in trouble should any fights or running occur. She made her way to the end of the walkway and stood in front of the second door. Ava and Eldon joined her and stood gingerly on the platform as it bowed slightly under the weight of all three of them.

"What do we do now? Eldon whispered.

"We knock," Mags said.

Both Eldon and Ava gave her confused and slightly incredulous looks. Mags smiled at them as she held up her fist and rapped on the door three times.

She heard movement inside, someone big. Mags took a half step back and readied herself. When the door opened, it wasn't the big woman standing there, but a small woman, blonde, but strong and regal. She smiled at Mags and stood aside, motioning for her to come in.

"That catwalk is a bit dodgy. Come on in. The floor of the rooms is much sturdier," she said.

Mags returned the smile and nodded. "Thank you." She stepped into the room. Eldon and Ava followed.

Inside, the big woman glared at them. She stood ready, her hand not quite on the hilt of her sword. Mags kept her hands clear of her weapons. She looked over at Eldon and Ava and was happy to see they were mirroring her, although from the nervous twitch of Ava's face and hands, Mags surmised pacifism was difficult for the girl to maintain.

The smaller woman held out a hand to Mags, which Mags took and shook.

"My name is Eir." She pointed to her companion. "You know Thora." From behind the big woman, two little faces peeked around her trunk-like legs. They grinned at Mags and stepped out. Thora pulled them to her and Mags noted they appeared to be very close in age, a boy and a girl. The smaller woman, Eir, went to them. "This is Hilde and Hagen."

"I'm Mags. This is Ava, Eldon, and Dane." Mags kept her smile in place but inside she felt a little pang of the beginnings of defeat. This was a family and they were running for a reason. Returning them to Angmere would likely mean their death.

Eir motioned toward a bench. "Please, sit. Would you like some tea as we work this out?"

Mags sat down on the bench and smiled. She motioned for the others to join her. "Thank you. Tea would be wonderful."

CHAPTER
TWENTY-EIGHT

Mags sipped her tea and relaxed. Dane had joined them in the room as there was no need to block the exit. Ava and Eldon stood by the door, still nervous someone would make a break for it. Mags let them. As long as they kept quiet everything would be fine.

Thora was still agitated. She sat on the bed with the children and glared at Mags. The children didn't seem scared at all. The little boy, Hagen, was about eight and big for his age, tall and sturdy, owing to an early growth spurt. He had the same blonde hair as Eir and her gray eyes. He followed Thora's lead and glared at Mags but kept looking up at Thora's face so as to stay aligned in distrust.

The little girl, Hilde, was a bit older, but not by much, perhaps ten. She was also tall, but wiry and strong. On her face there was only curiosity. She tilted her head as she looked Mags and the Trio over, and Mags smiled as she recognized the girl's careful, calm analysis of the group. She would be a formidable woman someday. Or at least she would be in places other than Norrik.

Hagen spoke first. "Are you taking us back to Uncle?"

"Hagen. No." Eir warned. She finished passing out mugs to the Trio, then sat beside Thora on the bed.

"We won't go," Hagen said, puffing out his chest. He looked up to Thora. "Will we?"

Thora hugged the boy close but said nothing as she dared Mags to argue.

"Well, I am bound to bring back a bounty," Mags said. Thora bristled. Eir put a hand on the big woman's thigh. They looked at each other, Eir smiling calmly and Thora looking panicked. "Why does Angmere want you so much?" Mags asked.

"My brother doesn't enjoy being told no," Eir said.

"No, no he doesn't," Mags agreed. "And what did he want that you denied?"

"I refused him my children and myself," Eir said.

"And they're not his?" Eldon asked. He had a wince on his face.

Ava scowled and smacked him. "Shut up, Eldon."

"No, they are definitely not," Eir said.

"My father was a great warrior!" Hagen yelled. He stood up and puffed out his chest. Thora pulled him back down.

"I'm sure he was," Mags said.

"Their father, my husband was a cunning warrior. And a fair and kind man." Eir smiled as the Trio stared at her in disbelief. "Yes, some Norrikmen are fair and kind, even to Rouslanders."

"He died of a fever shortly after Hagen was born. My father was also fair. A harsh man, but fair and not cruel. Angmere didn't inherit any of his good qualities. When Angmere took over, he didn't have the strength or cunning of our father. He promoted Ulf, who brought in that witch," Eir said. "She and Ulf convinced Angmere to name Hagen his heir. She also convinced him to provide Ulf a wife."

"The little girl?" Ava asked. Her face was red with rage.

"No, me," Eir said. "Angmere has promised Hilde to another group further north."

"You don't sell people," Dane said.

Eir shrugged. "Well, that's what dowries are. Most women have no choice."

"This one does," Thora said. "She won't be going anywhere she doesn't want to." She reached a big arm around both children.

Eir smiled up at Thora and kissed her cheek. The two women exchanged a look of determined love. Mags nodded at them.

"So you took off and headed south," Mags said. "Hoped to get lost in Kos?"

"We don't care where we get lost, just so long as we do," Thora said.

"And I complicate that," Mags said.

Thora glared, but Eir smiled as she looked Mags over. It was the same look her daughter had given Mags. Careful consideration.

"I suppose how complicated you make this depends on you," Eir said.

"It usually does," Mags agreed. "Well, even if I forget I ever saw you, Ulf is coming too. He won't let you go."

"How do you know he followed you?" Eir asked.

"He took your flight personally," Mags said. "I knew he wanted to be the one to find you."

"Yes. That sounds like him. He's never been one to let go of something he believes is his," Eir said. She snuggled closer to Thora.

"And clearly, you made a better choice," Mags said. She smiled at Thora. "He'll have you outnumbered. I think you blew all your coin on those dummies at Calen and the mercs you hired to scare me off in the alley. Right?"

"That's correct," Eir said. "You do seem rather determined. I wish I had hired you before Angmere did."

"I wish that too," Mags said. "So Geta, she's playing a

dangerous game with Matchi. Magic requires time, history, and ability. That little grub camp is no seat of magical power. She may have magic of some kind—I'm certainly no expert on that—but she's not a sorceress. She wants you back, but she doesn't want me to bring you back."

Eir looked thoughtful. "She's the one that arranged my marriage to Ulf, but I know they're together. She's ambitious."

"And stupidly so," Mags said. "She knows about the P'tak. I don't think she's from your North."

Thora spoke up. "What do you mean she doesn't want you to bring us back. She hired you."

Mags shook her head. "No . . . Well sort of yes, but no. I refused the job. She escalated things." She held up her arm. The blue spot glowed and as it did, it burnt her arm. Everyone in the room, except Mags, winced. "That's the mark of Matchi the Huntress. If this were just a matter of money, I would be able to back off. But with this?"

Eir nodded. "You're bound."

"I still don't get it. You can't die. What can this Matchi thing do to you?" Ava asked. Her tone was scoffing and suspicious.

"Ava, you saw her get tortured after she—" Dane said.

"No, we saw what happened after she lopped some poor schmuck's head off," Ava said.

"You cut somebody's head off?" Eldon asked, his eyes wide. "I thought you didn't kill people.

"I don't. That's not . . ." Mags stuttered. "Look, that witch, Geta, whatever she is, she thinks she's clever. She's made a deal with Matchi. If I don't bring you back, she'll have Matchi in a bind and in debt to her. She thinks that's a good thing, but trust me, it isn't. I don't like the idea of her gaining any kind of power."

Eir nodded. "No, she'll do something terrible with it. She's already done a lot of damage in Annik without magic. If she gets it, then we'll never be safe." She looked up at Thora and the two exchanged a look, then they both looked at Mags. "If something happens to us, promise me you'll make sure Hagen and Hilde are safe."

"You have my word on that," Mags said.

"What? We can't take them back to him!" Ava yelled. "Do you know what he'll do to them? Do you know what they'll do to the girl?"

"Yes, I know, but—" Mags tried to agree with them, but they came at her rapid-fire.

"Ulf will kill the boy," Dane said. "He'll kill Angmere and Hagen." The big kid stood up and went to stand next to the family. "I won't let that happen."

"I won't either," Ava said. She joined Dane and glared at Mags.

Eldon looked at Mags, then at Dane and his sister. He gulped and avoided Mag's eyes as he joined Dane and his sister.

Mags looked at Dane. "You know the consequences if they don't go back."

"Yeah, we do. And we don't care—" Ava yelled.

Mags held up a hand. Her eyes stayed locked on Dane's. He nodded.

"Ava. Eldon. I'm not the only one bound." Mags touched the mark on her arm. When she did, a small blue spot on each of the Trio's forehead glowed faintly. Just hot enough to annoy them. The red mark on Mag's face grew hot as well. "If I don't make sure they return to Annik, you all die."

"What?" Eldon gulped.

"It was Matchi's price to save you in the first place and make sure I do the job. If they don't return by Midsummer, you three die. And I'll have to be the one to do it."

Mags stood up. The Trio shuffled and fidgeted, nervous and frightened. But they didn't move. They remained in a protective circle around the little family.

"It doesn't change anything," Dane said. He looked to Ava and Eldon and they all agreed.

"Do what you have to do, but we're not going to let Angmere have them," Ava said.

The blue spot on Mags's arm sizzled and glowed and she winced as the pain intensified. She smiled through it. "All I have to do is deliver a bounty. If Angmere can't keep them, well, that won't be my problem."

Eir smiled at her. "Do you know anyone who might help smuggle a group south and provide protection services?"

Mags smiled back. She looked at the Trio. "You know, I just might."

CHAPTER
TWENTY-NINE

M ags sent Dane and Eldon back to the tavern to get the horses and gear while she and Ava helped Thora and Eir pack. When they returned, Jane was with them and Eldon looked to be in pain.

"You tried to ride," Mags said. She checked Duck's tack and the big horse nodded and whinnied at her.

"He's crazy," Eldon said, scowling at the horse.

"I told you not to do it," Dane said.

Mags laughed. "You got what you deserved." She checked Goose as well, but Dane had done a wonderful job. They trusted him and he adored them.

Thora, Eir, and the children came out of the flophouse. The kids cooed at the horses and showered Duck and Goose with scratches and affection. Mags put Hagen and Hilde on Duck and Eir on Goose.

"Oh so they can ride but I can't? They just met these people," Eldon groused as he rubbed his sore backside.

"Yeah. They can," Mags said. "They're children and I need to know they get clear fast if there's trouble." She looked to Dane. "You're with Goose. He'll protect her."

Dane nodded and stood next to Goose.

"So we're just going to take them back? This is a terrible plan," Ava said.

"We have to start back. We'll figure out the rest. I don't know. Stop bothering me!" She wasn't sure of a solid plan yet, but she at least had to have the intention of delivering a bounty. Mags finished her checks, then regarded Jane. "Until next time," she said, smiling.

"It's always a possibility this time was the last," Jane said. She grabbed Mags and kissed her like it was the last. When Jane let go of her, Mags was a little disoriented, but she shook her head to clear it and hugged Jane tight.

"There will always be a next time, even if it's a very long time. Take care of yourself, Janie."

Jane extracted herself and wiped the tears from her eyes but smiled. She didn't say anything else. She wrapped her shawl around herself and waved as she walked away. Mags felt a pang of familiar sadness, but she crushed it and sent it away. It was of no use to her, but even still, every time she left, it felt like a little part of her died. When she added up all those tiny pieces, she wondered how much of her was actually still alive.

The group started back north. If everything went just right and there were no delays, they would have enough time to get back to the enclave. They'd grab transport via the river north and that would help knock some time off the trip. It would be close, but they could still make it to Annik by Midsummer.

After about a day and a half, they were nearly to a river dock in the Arlean, when Mags got a funny feeling, one she had learned not to ignore. There were no other travelers. The road in either direction was clear. Odd for the road to one of the busier river ports. There was also a distinct lack of nature sounds—no birds, no squirrels, nothing save a silence that didn't match with the calm, bright sunny day. Mags stopped and listened. Thora picked up on it as well. The big woman drew her sword. Eldon and Ava were on Mags's right, on Duck's flank. Dane stood by Goose on her left. Thora was also to her left.

"Ambush," the big woman growled.

"It looks that way, yes," Mags said. She pulled her batons from their holsters and readied herself.

"Hagen. Hilde. Run. Hide. We'll find you." Eir stayed on Goose but pulled a sword. The children didn't question the order from their mother. The slid from Duck's back and disappeared into the underbrush behind them.

Ulf and six well-armed Norrik warriors stepped from the bushes in front of them. He held a leather bag in one hand and his great sword in the other.

"I'll take it from here, Darrish," Ulf said. "No need to go all the way back north." He smiled a mirthless smile at Eir. "Hello, wife. I'm pleased to see you're in good health."

"She's not your wife," Thora growled. She readied herself to fight him.

Ulf turned his head slowly and regarded her with a look of mocking disdain. He didn't answer her. He just laughed.

"I like it up north," Mags said. "I just love the smell of you Norrikmen. All fish and goat piss. You should bottle that scent and sell it at market." One of the warriors was close to Ava, two on Dane, and three trained on Mags herself. Ulf stood opposite Thora. They were definitely outnumbered. The Trio hadn't been exactly proven in battle, although Ava could fight and Dane was so big he could hold his own. Thora was a Norrik warrior, but seven on five was still bad odds.

Beside her, Ava was humming with anger. Rage rolled off the girl in waves. "We're not going anywhere with you," Ava said. She yanked her daggers from their sheaths and pointed at Ulf. "Come on then and try."

"I'll gut you and leave you for the crows," Ulf said. He turned his attention back to Mags. "Got something for you, Darrish." He held up the bag and grinned. "The fat brother didn't give us no trouble at all. He hated you. He'd a told me everything about you for free. Was happy when I told him I was after you. That sister, on the other hand, fought hard. Real scrapper, that one. Nearly took out Unger's eye." Ulf motioned to one of the Norrik. His face was marked with vicious scratches. "But in the end, she went the same way." Ulf turned over the bag and two heads fell out. There was no mistaking them. The red curls ruined in the dust.

It had been so long since Mags had felt such impotent rage that she hesitated, unable to unleash the fury that boiled up from within. Ava had no such problem. She screamed and threw a knife at Ulf's head. He caught it, then flung it back at her. The blade lodged in her shoulder. Ava screamed again, yanked it free and attacked the warrior in front of her.

Mags snapped out of her stunned lull as she was confronted the three Norrikmen in front of her. They came at her with their swords. To her left, Thora attacked Ulf, who laughed at her and deflected her sword with lazy parries and disrespect. The other two tackled Dane. Eldon jumped in to help him and the four formed a rolling scrum in the dirt.

Mags addressed her three attackers. They underestimated her, as men with swords usually did. They thrust their swords at her, expecting to break the wooden batons easily. But the batons were not meant for sword play. Mags used her quickness to sidestep the thrusts and in four quick blows, she had disarmed one of the men and broke both his arms. He screamed, and she hit him in the side of the jaw with both sticks. He crumped to the ground with blood pouring from his face.

The other two backed off when they saw their companion fall. Showing they were trained warriors and not totally stupid thugs, they flanked her and kept just out of reach of her batons. Beside her, Thora was tiring. Ulf's blows were fierce and the big woman did her best to parry, but Mags could see the exhaustion and fear in her face. She needed help.

Mags whistled to Duck. The huge warhorse snorted and whirled around so his rump faced her. Mags jumped up into the air and flipped over the attacker on her right. He had no time to turn around. Mags shoved him toward Duck, then she flattened herself on the ground. The horse gave a sort of battle cry of his own and kicked the Norrik warrior in the face, sending the man flying over Mags. She whistled again and Duck turned back around, his head now facing forward. He snorted and cried again, pleased with himself.

Mags popped up and smiled at him "Good boy." She then grinned and dealt with the last Norrikmen. She went for his kidneys, placing three quick blows to his sides. When he crumpled to his knees, she brought the batons down on his shoulders, then finished him with a blow to the back of the head.

Dane and Eldon had somehow pummeled their two attackers into unconsciousness. Ava stood over hers with bloody daggers in her hands and a horrified look on her face. Thora was spent. The big woman sucked in huge lung-fulls of air and could barely lift her sword. She had held her own. Ulf had a bloody nose and a wound in his side.

Mags stepped in front of her. He blue hand burned but remained a hand. "I'm going to pay you back triple for what you did."

Ulf's face contorted with rage as he realized his advantage had evaporated. To Mags, the next ten seconds seemed as long as her entire three hundred plus years of life. Ulf grabbed Goose's neck rein. The big horse rolled his eyes and flattened his ears back. He turned his head and bit a hunk out of Ulf's shoulder. Ulf screamed and dropped the rein, then he thrust his broadsword into Goose's chest, just behind his leg. The horse shrieked in pain and crumpled to the ground. Ulf tried to pull Eir down from the saddle before the horse fell, but he wasn't quick enough. He jumped back, avoiding the big body, but Eir was crushed under the weight of the horse.

161

Mags, Dane, and Thora all screamed at the same time as they watched the horse and the woman flounder. Ulf took off into the bushes. Mags felt her face flush and the red mark on her cheek burn as she considered giving chase, but the screams of her companions brought her back to the fallout at hand.

Thora pulled Eir free. Mags went to her first. Eir's chest heaved as the woman struggled to breathe. Blood bubbled at her lips. Her chest and pelvis were crushed. Thora cried and cradled her in her lap. Hagen and Hilde screamed as they burst from the forest and ran to their mother's side. Eir weakly raised a hand to each child's face and whispered calm words of love to them. She did the same to Thora, who could do nothing but sob. Eir would die in minutes.

Beside them, Goose squealed and snorted in pain. A great puddle of blood pooled around him and his eyes were all whites with fear and pain. Dane knelt in the dirt and cried. Mags shoved him out of the way and examined the wound. Fat tears streamed down her face as she fought the realization that she could do nothing to help him. She laid a hand on his head and cooed to him. "Easy, friend. Easy. I'm here."

Goose quieted when he heard her voice. His eyes locked onto hers and Mags's heart broke harder than she would have ever thought possible as she read love and trust, fighting the pain in the horse's big brown eyes.

Mags looked to the little family, then back at Goose. She closed her eyes and screamed.

"TORMENT!"

THIRTY

A loud screeching sound, like nails on a slate filled the air. Everyone but Mags coved their ears and winced. Mags didn't bother. She knew it wouldn't help. The painful frequency vibrated her eardrums and induced a splitting headache immediately. After a few seconds, the smell of purification and burning sulfur filled the air. Everyone choked on it and covered their nose. Except Mags. She knew it couldn't be shut out.

"Torment, show yourself! There's no time for your games!" Mags yelled.

Green mist appeared and a slight man with gleeful black eyes and sharp pointed teeth stepped out of it. His long black hair was wild and stood up at all angles and his clothes were black leather. He hissed and laughed.

"Maggie!" He looked around at the chaos and clapped. Delighted. "Now this is a party!"

"Save them. Both of them. I'll take it. Double." Mags stood up and set her jaw.

Torment stopped dancing. He stared at Mags and his smile widened. "No. Not both. You choose."

"I can take it. Just save them both."

"Oh I know you can handle the pain. That's easy. But you know what's more delicious? What's delectable?"

Mags's face contorted with anger. Torment had always been cruel, but this was a new low for him. "No, I won't choose. Both."

Torment shrugged. "Oh, okay, well then neither." He laughed at her rage. "You have to choose."

Except it wasn't a choice. It was clear what she had to do. Mags knelt beside the horse. She petted him, then bent her head low and put her forehead against his cheek. Goose snorted at her and gave her a soft nicker even in his pain. Tears streamed down Mags's face as she stood up. She walked over to the family. They looked up at her, devastation and grief on all their faces. Mags nodded to Torment. "Do it."

Torment walked around Mags, sniffing her. His face was that of a glutton inhaling the scent of some gourmet delight. "The pain here is so wonderful. So decadent. And it's only an appetizer," he purred. "I can't wait for the main dish."

Torment tiptoed and danced gleefully over to Eir. He leaned down close to her. The children recoiled from him. They scooted as close to Thora as they could. Thora's face contorted in disgust and fear, but she held Eir, refusing to let her go.

"Don't you touch her," Thora growled.

"That won't be necessary," Torment hissed. He moved inches from her face and inhaled. He sucked in great breaths, more air than any human could, and as he did, colored wisps of dank greens and grays swirled around Eir. He sucked them in and as they disappeared into his mouth and up his nostrils, Eir healed. Her crushed chest and pelvis knitted themselves back together. The color returned to her face and life-fueling air again flowed freely as she breathed. Eir grasped at Thora and looked confused. Thora helped her stand and the children wrapped themselves around her. Thora steadied her and looked to Mags.

"H-How?"

"Oh you'll see," Torment replied. He skipped over to Mags, twirled, tilted his head at her, then waited.

Mags took a deep breath and nodded.

Torment's face turned from irreverent, gleeful trickster to hateful monster. His teeth elongated into irregular sharp shards and his eyes turned black, rimmed in red with black inky streaks that resembled the mottling of rotting flesh. He hissed, then pounced on her, shoving her to the ground. He knelt on her chest and lowered his hideous maw to her mouth and kissed her. Through his open mouth, all of pain and ruin flowed into Mags. She felt her stomach distend as it filled her. When he had exhaled all of it into her, his face returned to normal and he got up from her chest. Mags didn't move. She lay still, bloated and miserable as she waited. The worst was coming.

If someone would have asked her to describe it, she supposed she would have said it was like tasting every putrid thing in the world and then smelling every terrible smell in existence as somebody broke every single bone in your body right before they set you on fire.

That was the easy part.

After that, the whispers started.

The voices told her terrible things. The insults and accusations grew louder and louder. They filled her ears and soon they drowned out all other sounds, save for the screams of agony. Thousands of voices, screaming in pain and rage and fear all echoed in her head. Mags's screams soon joined them as the pain started. Her flesh burned and seared, then it felt like stab wounds pierced her all over. Her muscles all cramped at once and her body twisted and twitched at unnatural angles as her bones cracked over and over and over. It felt like something tore its way into her stomach and ripped out organs, but all she could feel was the pain because she didn't dare open her eyes. It went on for what seemed like days and she lost any sense of time, space, or self. There was only torment.

But it didn't last forever and the pain waned. The screams quieted as if they had moved off into the distance and the hateful voices returned to whispers. When Mags opened her eyes, Torment beamed and clapped.

"Bravo! That was exquisite! Magdalena, you are without a doubt, my favorite—"

"Shut up," Mags growled as she heaved herself over onto her stomach and crawled over to Goose. He was almost gone. He'd managed to open his eyes when he sensed Mags, but he could no longer move. He gave a weak snort and closed his eyes. Mags sobbed.

From behind her a deep voice spoke. "I'll do it. I'll take it. Please. Help him," Dane said.

Mags looked up at him and shook her head. "Kid, you don't know what this is. You can't—"

"I can take it. Is there any rule that says I can't?" Dane asked.

"You'll suffer. Like you've never suffered before," Mags said. "Physical strength isn't the only thing required."

Dane nodded. "I understand."

"No, no, you don't. It will change you. You think it's only a few minutes, but it will feel like much longer, and you won't be able to shut it out. Not even after."

Dane ignored her. He addressed Torment. "I accept. Save him."

"Done," Torment squealed. He galloped over to the horse in a grotesque childish mockery. He sucked in every ounce of pain from the huge animal. When he tackled Dane, he was even more violent and terrifying than he had been with Mags. Dane's face paled, then reddened as he inhaled all of Goose's agony.

Eldon and Ava screamed as they watched their friend twist and writhe. Mags had never seen it before. The big kid screamed until he was hoarse and after that his screams were harsh, high-pitched sounds that strained human vocal chords past any limit imaginable.

Beside her, Goose struggled. The horse seemed to feel Dane's pain but he thrashed as his wounds healed. Mags tried to calm him, but the horse got to his feet, agitated and wild. Mags stood up and grabbed him to quiet him, but he reared and ignored her.

Dane screamed. "I-I can't! It's . . . It's so . . . much."

When he cried out, Torment laughed. He waved his hand and both Dane and Goose screamed. The black cloud of pain and putrescence exited Dane and flowed back into Goose. The gigantic horse reared one last time, then he collapsed to the ground, dead.

Mags screamed and threw herself down near Goose, frantic to stop the bleeding, to help, but it was no use. Goose was gone.

Dane crawled to them. His eyes were dark and bloodshot, with great black circles under them. He leaned against Goose's neck and whispered to the horse. When he raised his head, his eyes found Mags and tears streamed down his face. "I'm sorry. I-I-I couldn't."

Mags didn't have the words to comfort him. In her mind she knew it wasn't his fault. Normal humans couldn't withstand Torment. Still, in that moment, Mags couldn't bring herself to tell him it was alright. She couldn't bring herself to say anything at all.

CHAPTER
THIRTY-ONE

Torment danced around her, gleeful. He clapped and sang. "Everything about that entire sequence was magnificent! I'm not sure I've ever had something as delicious as that. You really know how to suffer, Magdalena! And this big boy"—Torment knelt next to Dane and grabbed his face, smooshing his cheeks like an auntie overcome by an adorable child—"he almost made it. I thought he was going to but he just couldn't quite reach the finish. Don't fret, big fella, very few humans can do what Magdalena here does. There's nothing for you to be sorry about." Torment looked down at Goose and smirked. "Well, except for your dead horse."

Mags snarled and lunged for him. Torment laughed and disappeared, leaving behind the disgusting smelling green mist.

"Until next time, Maggie-Ole-Girl . . ."

Mags screamed in rage and frustration and grief. She found Thora's sword in the dust and raged as she hacked at a stout elm. She slashed and bit at the wood, hoping with each blow it would dull the sense of loss, of Jane, of Goose. She raged against the tree until it cracked and toppled down. She'd had enough. Enough of these Norrikmen, enough of bounty hunting, enough of Harvests, and enough of the accursed gods. When the tree was splinters and the sword a useless, bent hunk of steel, Mags stopped. She stood there beside the road, out of breath but not physically tired, just emotionally spent.

She turned around and looked at the party. Dane cried as he lay in the dirt beside Goose's body. He had gone from broad-shouldered, broad-chested hunk to a rickety, tired figure, stooped and frail, yet his physical body hadn't changed at all. Eldon, Thora, Eir, and the children all looked terrified of her, and Ava stood over the dead body of one of the Norrikmen, her hands covered in blood.

Mags said nothing to any of them. She threw down the ruined sword, then she found the leather bag. Gently as she could she gathered Eddie and Jane's heads. She took them into the forest and buried them. Mags knelt beside Jane's mound and cried. She didn't know how long she'd sat there, but after a while she heard a voice behind her.

"No."

"You," Mags spat. She looked up to the sky and screamed at the disembodied voice. "You can go straight to hell and take those three with you. If it wasn't for you and for them, everything would be fine. Goose wouldn't be dead. Jane would be alive. I'd be shut of Norrikmen and done with all this death!"

"No . . ."

"Shut up with that word! I don't care what you want! I don't care about them! I don't care about any of them!"

"Magdalena, we both know that is a lie." Kohoc the Harvester stepped from behind a large tree. The black mist trailed him. He drew close to Mags and sighed as he looked down at her. "Do you know what I thought when I first saw you?"

"Kohoc . . ."

"I thought it was such a shame, such a waste to have to harvest someone as kind as you." He reached out and tipped her chin up. "You can't see the people you harvest like I can. I see their whole lives before I take them. I see their kindness, their joy, their love, and their innocence. Most of the time, there's nothing evil or deserving of death about them. I never know why they're to be harvested. Mother probably doesn't either. But I suppose that's life. Anyway, I saw you very clearly that day, so young, full of life, kind and gentle, to that beast of Matchi's even. I hated the thought of harvesting your soul. But more, I hated what you would become if Matchi had her way with you. I thought for sure if you saw all that death, brought it to the innocent, you'd curdle like milk in the sun. But you didn't. You're still kind and gentle, and you can't help but try and save the little things that need saving. You're not rage. You're not death." He took her blue hand and held it up. "This did not change you. Do you understand what a rare gift that is?"

"It's not a gift. It's a curse. To feel is a curse," Mags said.

"No. To feel nothing—no pain, no grief, no love, that is a curse. But to feel it all, as awful as it may be sometimes, is a blessing. I didn't give it to you. No god anywhere did. You had it. You've kept it. And to me, it's beautiful and amazing."

"You wouldn't say that if you had to—"

He stopped her. "But I do. I do have to. I've taken souls beyond count and I can tell you that the feeling is what honors them."

"I-I don't think I can keep going," Mags said. "I don't have enough time. I-I can't—"

"If you don't keep going, if you don't complete this task, those three die. It's that simple and you know Matchi, it really will be that simple," Kohoc said. "That voice, it's their mother."

Mags nodded. "I know. I saw her in a dream."

"That's a powerful thing, that kind of love. That woman has fought hard to keep it and she's trusting you."

"I don't want it."

Kohoc tilted his head and gave her a hint of a smile. "Yes, you do."

"I don't have time. If I go back north, I'm outnumbered and I know that bastard is going to be waiting to jack me and take—"

Kohoc nodded. "Yes. Those are all problems. In three hundred years I've seen you solve worse."

Mags looked at him. Kohoc the Harvester was feared. He was death. He was dark and sallow and mirthless and kind and wise. He had never failed to help her, even when he didn't have to. He was her family. Just like Andie, and Elio, and Raylon and Fallon, and Jane, and Duck and Goose. And the Trio of idiots. She loved them all and she wasn't about to let any of the down.

Probably.

A spark of hope kindled in her heart. She looked up at Kohoc.

"I'm going to need a big favor."

CHAPTER
THIRTY-TWO

That's not going to be possible," Kohoc said.

"You're the only one who can make it possible," Mags replied. "You know that I have to ensure they go back." She held up her arm brand.

"Yes. So take them back and let Matchi deal with it," Kohoc said. He crossed his arms and scowled at her, which was not a whole lot different from his happy look.

"No. I'm going to deal with it. Add on a hundred more Harvests. I don't care. Just please, help me."

Kohoc stared at her a moment. His sad eyes somehow got sadder. "I wanted that peace for you."

"Will it be peace?" Mags asked.

"You'll know when you know," Kohoc said. "What do you need?"

"Something Matchi will send the hound for. Something that will make her very unhappy should she find it missing," Mags said. "But something small, easily concealable."

If it were possible for Kohoc to feel amusement, Mags thought she had just seen it pass his face. His thin, gray lips twitched as if they wanted to break into a smile. "I think I know what that might be." He took a step backward and black mist began to swirl around him. "I'll return." He pulled his black hood over his head and as the dark fog enveloped him, he disappeared.

Mags returned to the group. They busied themselves making a camp off the road in a stand of trees. Dane was weak and dazed. Eldon nervous and overly helpful. Thora and Eir held the children and each other close. They were still in an emotional state of disbelief. Eventually the camp was functional and the fight area tidied up. It forced everyone to sit around and think about the next move.

"What are we going to do?" Ava asked. Her voice was quiet and there was no trace of her usual attitude. She'd kept quiet since the fight, helping Mags tie up the Norrikmen that Ulf had left behind. Ava hadn't been able to look at the one she'd killed. Mags had moved the body off the road on the opposite side of the camp. Ava had cleaned the blood from her hands, but she kept looking at them, then rubbing them on her pants, as if some stain still lingered.

Mags poured herself some tea and sat next to Dane. "We're all going to go back to the Annik enclave."

"Are you insane? Angmere will kill us all. Especially now," Eldon said.

"Angmere isn't the danger. Ulf is," Thora said. "Him and that witch."

Eir nodded and leaned against Thora. "He'll come for us again before we can reach the enclave. You gave him a bloody nose. He won't forget it."

"No, he won't. But he won't attack us again unless he's sure of better odds," Mags said.

"He definitely won't attack with you here," Eir said.

"We're going to split up. Ava and I will go ahead. We'll take Thora, and a bag of heads. Dane and Eldon, you're going to stay with Eir and the children."

"A bag of heads?" Thora asked.

"Half-bounty," Mags said. "Heads are easy to get."

Eir smiled. "They won't fall for that trick, although Angmere is dumb."

"I know," Mags said. "And Ulf will hang back. Wherever he is, he's lurking around the roads waiting to follow us north."

"If we split up, what's to stop him from killing me and Eldon?" Dane asked.

"I'll bargain with him," Eir said. "He'll want me alive. You're part of the deal."

"Also, I think he's cocky and he'll want a big finish," Mags said.

"He has always wanted to skin us," Eldon said. Ava and Dane all nodded in agreement.

"But that still leaves us outnumbered and in their house," Ava said.

Mags nodded. "In their house, yes. Outnumbered, well, let's hope not."

It was all a big gamble. They were right, if Ulf decided not to bargain and Dane and Eldon died, then there would be no plan. Mags, Ava, and Thora would be trapped. But three hundred years of chasing down every manner of person had taught Mags many things, and one of them was that men like Ulf never ever believed they could lose. They were overconfident and felt entitled to their victory. He didn't see Dane or Eldon as threats. She'd seen it that first night. She'd seen it in the fight they'd just had. He'd agree to take them back and torture them, probably in front of Mags. Bullies could never resist showing off.

"We don't have any allies," Ava said. "How can we possibly not be outnumbered?"

"Well maybe you don't have any allies, but I still have a few."

THIRTY-THREE

The night passed uneventfully. Ava hadn't woken her for second watch, but Mags didn't sleep anyway. She found Ava across the road, staring at the body of the man she'd killed. Mags let her be. She remembered that feeling, the guilt that plagued you after you'd killed for the first time. It couldn't have happened to a person less equipped to handle it. Ava was a seething ball of rage with a conscience. When reminded of her humanity, she lashed out. It made Mags feel uneasy. She couldn't help the girl unless the girl wanted to be helped. Ava never wanted to be helped.

So Mags had left her alone and checked out the other direction until morning came. They broke camp and packed up. Dane helped her saddle Duck.

"Kohoc is the key?" Dane asked.

"No. Eldon is," Mags said.

"Eldon?" Dane looked over at his friend, who struggled to put out the campfire. "Are you sure?"

"Quite sure," Mags said. "Go slow. Ulf will come for you. Don't resist or give him any reason to kill you."

"Yeah, don't worry about that, but umm, seriously? Eldon?"

"He can do it. As long as Kohoc—" Mags looked past Dane and saw the familiar black cloud appear. Kohoc stepped out of the mist with an unusual spring in his step and the barest hint of a smile on his face. "You got it?" Mags asked him.

His gaunt, pale face had two little red points on his cheeks. For Kohoc, that was flush with excitement. His eyes sparkled and he held out a green gem that hung from a delicate silver chain. It caught the morning light and glistened like dew on a leaf in the forest.

"Oh, she's definitely going to be mad about this," Mags said. She took the gem and admired it.

"Yes, my sister is petty," Kohoc said. "I would have never believed theft to be so stimulating, but—"

"She deserves it," Mags finished.

"She does," Kohoc said. He realized Mags caught him enjoying something and he became morose and serious again. "I hope this plan of yours works, Magdalena." He looked around at the party: the Trio, Eir and Thora, the children. "They will all suffer if it doesn't."

Mags nodded. She didn't have words to retort. He was right. They would. They would suffer and die. And it would be her fault. "Thank you," she said. Mag pointed to Goose's body. They just didn't have time to deal with the big horse, not the way Mags wanted. "One more favor, can you make sure he . . ."

Kohoc nodded. He closed his eyes and Goose's body was gone. "He's peaceful."

Mags sobbed. Kohoc put a hand on her shoulder and let her. Then he seemed to realize everyone in the camp could see him and he straightened up and tried to look grave. Kohoc yanked his hood over his head. With his face covered, it softened as he looked at her, a look of fatherly affection. "This is a reckless plan. Everyone here is in serious trouble. But you know what? They have the best chance they could with you." He stepped backward into the black mist and was gone.

Mags finished crying and wiped her eyes. "Eldon, come here." Mags held up the green gem.

Eldon stared at the gemstone and whistled. He grinned. "That's got to be worth a fortune!" He reached for it.

Mags pulled it back out of his reach. "It's worth a great deal but to only one person."

"No way. If we sell that thing we can buy an army and go flatten Angmere and Ulf!"

"You won't get that far. You don't want to be caught with this necklace. If Matchi finds you with it instead of Ulf, she'll kill you. This is a very important job. When Ulf captures you, you need to plant this on him as soon as you can. He cannot know you did it. Do you understand?"

"I mean, easy as pie, but I still think we should sell it," Eldon said.

Mags grabbed his ear and twisted it. "Listen to me very carefully. We are all depending on you. Plant the necklace on him. Don't get cute or mouth off to him so he guts you before you do it."

Eldon squawked but nodded. "Okay, okay. I get it. Why does Ulf get it?"

"Because it's going to ensure our backup finds us," Mags said. She let go of his ear, then patted his shoulder. "I'm betting on you. Don't let me down."

Eldon beamed at her. "I won't."

CHAPTER

THIRTY-FOUR

They'd stopped at a smaller town and bought horses. She'd left Duck with Dane when they'd parted ways just after they'd crossed back into Mirrik. It had been hard to leave him. The horse was uneasy and upset at his missing companion, and he didn't want to leave Mags.

"I know. I don't want to leave you either, but I need you to take care of Dane and Eldon. Don't let them do anything dumb."

Duck seemed to sigh in horse, but Mags knew he understood. He quieted and stood beside Dane.

After they'd split, Mags, Ava, and Thora made slow time north.

"Don't you think we're moving too slow? We'd get there faster if we took a barge," Ava said.

"Yes. I do think we're moving slowly. We need to. I want them to get ahead of us."

"That's stupid. What if they ambush us?" Ava asked.

"No. Ulf won't confront us before we get to the enclave. He knows he can't win any fight unless we're cornered." So many things needed to line up. Eldon had to do his part. Dane had to keep Eldon quiet and steady everyone, Mags had to sell the ruse with Thora, and Matchi had to care enough about what was stolen from her to track it down. It was a lot of moving parts and of them all, Mags herself controlled only one. She swallowed hard and sighed, giving in fully to the idea that she needed people. It was awful and uncomfortable, but it was what had to be done.

Thora agreed. "He's a coward. He'll wait until he's sure we can't win."

"I hope you know what you're doing," Ava said.

"So do I," Mags said.

THEY REACHED the Annik enclave in a leisurely week. Mags stopped about ten miles out and tied Thora's hands loosely to sell the gambit. They were met with jeers, all directed at Thora. The big woman rode stoically as Norrikmen hurled insults and garbage at her. Ava snarled at them, but they ignored her. Thora was clearly the sport they desired.

Inside the feast hall, Angmere held court. He was in a jovial mood as he ate and gulped down wine. Geta sat to his right. She sipped from a goblet and smiled at Mags when they entered.

"My lord, the Bounty Hunter has returned," Geta purred.

"Not a complete bounty," Angmere said. There was mocking tone to his voice.

Mags suppressed an eyeroll. They believed they had laid the cleverest of traps for her and while that was exactly what she wanted them to believe, it was still difficult to stomach the supposed superiority of idiots. She held up a burlap bag. "Oh, I got them both." In reality, the head in the bag belonged to the dead Norrikmen. It was a rotting mess and unrecognizable. "I'm fine with half payment for this one."

"Why would I pay you anything?" Angmere said. He ripped a

chunk of meat from a chicken and shoved it in his mouth, then washed it down with red wine.

"You contracted me. Standard bounty is half for the head. And you never specified alive," Mags said.

"No, I mean why would I pay you for some rotting hunk of meat? My sister's head is not in that bag." He chugged his wine and held the cup out for more. "She's alive. I suppose not well," he said.

From the side door, Ulf entered. He had Eir by the arm. Her hands were bound. One large warrior carried both Hagen and Hilde, who kicked and bit at him for all they were worth. Two more warriors entered shoving a bound and gagged Eldon and Dane ahead of them.

Ulf smirked. "Looks like you lose all around, Darrish."

Mags dared not smile, but her heart pounded at seeing Dane and Eldon alive. However, her heart stopped when she saw Eldon's hand. His right hand was a bloody, crumpled mess. Someone had beaten it until it no longer resembled a human hand, but rather a misshapen blob on the end of Eldon's skinny arm.

Ulf smirked at her. "I suppose it was the best trick a woman could think of," he said. "Splitting up. Trying to pass off that big bitch and whatever rotting head is in that bag as a proper bounty."

"It did seem like a clever idea at the time," Mags replied. Her blue hand itched and burned. She thought of Goose and Jane and she ached to make Ulf suffer.

"Well, you're only a woman, and you're Darrish, so it's to be expected." Ulf laughed. All the men laughed as well, and Angmere nearly choked he laughed so hard. "I'm going to kill them all slowly," he said. "I'll gut them and make you watch, then I'll butcher your other horse and tan its hide for new boots."

Mags began to vibrate with rage. She flexed her hand and the

180

red mark on her cheek scorched her skin. Ulf saw it and laughed harder.

"Ulf tells us Eir was crushed. What sorcery saved her?" Geta asked.

"Oh you're going to find out firsthand," Mags replied. "I promise."

"Enough of this. Are we skinning some people or what?" Angmere belched and wiped his mouth on his filthy sleeve. "Let's at least gut these Rousland twats. Bring me my sword!"

The Norrikmen grabbed Ava, Dane, and Eldon. They shoved them down on their knees as a servant brought Angmere his blade. He unsheathed it and pointed at each of them. "Which one first? I think maybe you," he said as he pointed at Ava.

Mags watched the selection process calmly. She controlled her anger and as she did, her heart beat steady in her chest. When she felt the second heartbeat, faint at first, then louder and stronger as it drew near, she smiled.

From outside the hall came the frightened screams of seasoned Norrik warriors. The solid oak doors crashed in and the hall was filled with the long, angry bray of a hound who had found his quarry.

The hound's heartbeat merged with hers and the animal stopped at Mag's side. He stared directly at Ulf. The hound's lip curled up and he bared his teeth.

Mags's vision blurred, then a red tinge washed over it. She growled and bared her teeth as well. The hound coiled up his back legs and sprang at Ulf, knocking him to the ground and pinning him there. Ulf's eyes went wild with fear as the great beast growled in his face.

Mags put a foot on Ulf's chest. "You have something that doesn't belong to you," she said.

Before he could answer the room was lit by a brilliant blue flash. Matchi the Huntress appeared. Her silver bow was drawn and an arrow notched.

"This place again? I just got the smell out of my hair!" she yelled. "How did a fish-licker like you steal from me?" She trained her arrow at Ulf.

He panicked and squirmed, but Mags and the hound held him. "I-I don't know what you're talking about. I didn't steal anything!"

"It's in his left pocket," Eldon said.

Mags smiled. She reached down and pulled the green gemstone necklace from Ulf's pocket. She held it out to Matchi, who snatched it from her hand.

"How could he have possibly gotten this?" She pressed the tip of the arrow into Ulf's temple. "Where did you get this?"

"I don't know! I swear! I didn't steal anything from you!"

"Possession is 90 percent of the law," Mags said. The hound growled beside her in agreement.

"Still it's curious," Matchi said. She looked at Mags and narrowed her eyes. But then, she shrugged. "Oh well." Without looking, she put the arrow through Ulf's stomach.

Mags knelt beside him and stared at him as he choked and sputtered. He grabbed at his guts but she pulled his hands back and held them. She smirked down at him. "Still think it was just an okay plan?"

Ulf twitched and struggled but she held him fast. "No, hang on. Struggle. Make it last," she said. "You deserve the best."

A great bubble of blood burbled up from Ulf's mouth.

"Wait, don't go just yet." Mags closed her eyes. "Kohoc?"

Her hand burned, but she didn't care. She smiled and welcomed the pain as the cobalt sickle, the bane of her existence for over three hundred years appeared. For the first time, she didn't dread it or hate it. She held it up and admired it as the light bounced off it and showed beautiful patterns in its blue steel-like qualities.

When she looked down at Ulf, he was terrified. His eyes had gone wide and he blubbered and pleaded. "I'm sorry, please."

Mags smiled at him. "I don't deal in repentance, that's someone else's department. I told you I'd repay you. For my horse and for Jane." With a backhand sweep of the sickle, Mags cut off Ulf's head. It remained severed. With her other hand, she reached down and grabbed it. His eyes still twitched and they still seemed to hold terror in them. The hound brayed again and Mags threw Ulf's head into the fireplace. Her hand returned to its human form, painlessly. Another gift from Kohoc.

"For once," Mags said, "that felt good."

CHAPTER
THIRTY-FIVE

The room was silent, then Matchi spoke.

"Well, that was dramatic," she said. "I think maybe I'm proud of you, Magdalena. Okay then, who dies next?" She whirled to judge the rest; an arrow notched in her bow.

It was then that the panic sunk in, and the Norrik warriors all scrambled to leave the hall. Matchi shook her head. She waved a hand and all the doors sealed. The hound came to her right. Mags stood on her left.

The Norrikmen all huddled in a corner. Angmere stared at the headless body of his second. He sobered quickly and trembled with fear. "Wha-what happened?"

"He had my property," Matchi said. "That's what happens when you steal from me. Doesn't your old man god punish theft? That figures. Probably too busy stinking of fish."

"Great Huntress, we understand Ulf's transgression, however, what of your hound's unfulfilled bounty?" Geta approached. She slithered and hissed like a snake.

"Unfulfilled bounty?" Mags shook her head. "No. It's complete."

"You did not return the two women as promised," Geta said. For the first time, her voice waivered and squeaked from her throat. "Did we not bargain, Mighty Huntress?"

"We did," Matchi said. She waved her hand and the blue mark on Mag's arm burned. "Magdalena?"

"The bounty stands. I tracked them. I made sure they were returned. Are they not both here now?"

Matchi looked to Eir and Thora. "Is it them? Wow, that's a big woman," Matchi said as she eyed Thora.

"Ulf brought back Eir," Geta said. "You tried to pass off a rotting head as her."

"Magdalena?"

Mags's arm burned hotter.

"Ow! They're both back here. I made sure of it. You didn't specify the means," Mags yelled.

Geta's face reddened with rage.

Matchi looked thoughtful for a moment, then she smiled and nodded. "Agreed. The contract is fulfilled."

She inclined her head at Geta. "Now. Give me what you promised. The location of the Black Archer."

Geta's face changed from red to white and her eyes widened. "No, no. It cannot be fulfilled. Your Hound didn't perform the task. I don't have to honor this agreement!"

Mags nudged Matchi's shoulder. "She doesn't know the location of The Black Archer. She's not a sorcerer."

Eir stepped forward. "She's a charlatan. A fake."

Matchi sneered at Geta. "You tried to trick me?"

The great hound beside her growled and lowered his haunches as he coiled himself to spring again.

Geta screamed and pleaded. "No, please, Great Goddess, Huntress, I beg you. I did no such thing. I-I—"

The hound grabbed Geta by the throat and shook her back and forth. The entire room heard Geta's spine snap several times. The hound dropped her body at Matchi's feet.

Both Matchi and Mags smiled at him. "Good Boy," they said in unison.

Matchi looked around the room. "This is a disgusting place," she said. She gave the hound a hand signal. He sat at her side. Matchi pointed at Mags. "Next time, don't involve me with these matters. Stay south, where you belong." Matchi touched her necklace. "There are a precious few who could have taken this necklace. That fish-licker wasn't one of them. But one of the ones who could have pulled it off has a pathetic soft spot for you. Care to comment?"

Mags shrugged. "Not really, no."

Matchi stared at her. Her eyes narrowed, but she said nothing.

The hound padded over to Mags and licked her on the face. She smiled at him and scratched behind his ear. "Thanks, old friend. I owe you one."

He licked her again, then went back to sit beside his mistress. Both Huntress and hound vanished in a blinding blue light.

CHAPTER
THIRTY-SIX

Mags and the Trio escorted Thora, Eir, and the children south. Without Ulf and the pretense of a magic user, Angmere couldn't hope to hold power for long. Mags extracted her bounty from him before they left the enclave. She split it into four equal shares and distributed it to the Trio. The Norrikmen were all terrified of Mags so they kept clear and didn't resist when Eir declared they were leaving.

One evening as they camped at the border of Norrik and Mirrik, Ava posed a question.

"Why not stay here?" Ava asked. "Angmere is done."

Eir shook her head. "There will always be another Ulf. I grew up here. I've seen it time and time again. If I stay, I'll never hold power, not even for my son. He'd be in danger, and I don't know if I could prevent him from becoming something I hate. Nothing would change for my daughter either. I don't want this for them."

"But it's your home," Eldon said.

Eir grasped Thora's hand and smiled at her. "No, it isn't. Not anymore."

They followed the Summer Trades back the way they came,

stopping in Calen to check on Raylon and Fallon, then fording the river at Sheaf. From there it was an easy trip to Watchpoint.

ON THE DOCKS AT WATCHPOINT, they said their goodbyes. Eir, Thora, and the children had booked passage on a ship bound for Kos.

"Still feel like you need to get lost there?" Mags asked.

"No. Just want to see it. I never thought I'd ever see anything outside of Norrik. Angmere can't get to us anyway. He can't afford it." Eir jingled her coin purse and smiled. "So there's the matter of payment for delivering us here."

Eldon and Ava perked up at the mention of money. "Ah, sure what do you think is the going rate for—ow!" Eldon rubbed the back of his head where Mags smacked him.

"Keep it. You'll need it for a fresh start," Mags said.

Dane pulled out his share of the bounty and handed it to Eir. "Find your children some place quiet. Some place nice."

Ava looked thoughtful and a bit sour, but she nodded. She handed over her share as well.

Eldon looked at the two of them as if they had grown a tail and three additional heads. "But I was gonna buy a horse. And my hand." He held up his hand. Mags had set it and wrapped it. It would take time to heal but he would be fine. His sister and Dane glared at him and finally he relented. He handed his bag to the children. "Fine."

They shook hands with Thora and Eir and watched them board the ship. Hagen and Hilde waved to them from the deck as the ship got underway. Once they were far enough out to sea, Mags turned to the Trio.

"Well, I got my money back. You're safe from Norrik raiders. Probably. If you can stay that way is a different story, but you're good for now."

"What do you mean?" Ava asked.

"I mean Matchi won't kill you. You can go anywhere you like." Mags gave them each ten bronze. "There. Now you're not completely broke."

Dane stared at the coins in the palm of his hand. Duck walked up beside him and nudged him. Dane reached under the horse's neck and rubbed him. He handed the money back to Mags. "Just keep it all together. If I need it, I'll ask."

Ava stared at him. She didn't give the money back. "Dane, you're sure?"

"I'm staying," he said quietly. "If that's okay?" he asked Mags.

She smiled at him. "Yeah. Sure. You're a good hand with horses."

Eldon pocketed the money. "I'll stay too. It's obvious you need me," he said.

"Clearly," Mags said dryly as she rolled her eyes. She looked to Ava.

A strange look passed over the girl's face. Mags read conflict there. Pride. Detachment. Pain. Fear. And the tiniest glimmer of admiration. "Yeah, sure. Fine. Until something better comes along."

"Naturally," Mags said. She turned and started down a side street. The Trio followed.

"Where are we going?" Ava asked.

"Villein's office. Maybe we can pick up some work," Mags said.

"Like bounties and stuff?" Eldon asked. "I mean, what about protection jobs? Hey, where's a good tavern? I bet I could double this money in no time." He danced around her, hopping on one leg as he spat out suggestions for employment.

"We'll keep an eye out for any good job," Mags said.

"Hey! You know what? I'm going to buy a horse!"

Mags shook her head. "No, you're not."

Eldon was undeterred. He ignored her and began describing his ideal mount in vivid detail. "A sleek white pacer. No fast . . . No, one of those horses that jumps."

Mags closed her eyes and tuned out the rambling, non-stop word salad as they headed off to find the Villein. Dane kept pace beside her with Duck. Ava walked ahead, lost in her own feelings. Mag stared at her and debated about how to tell her what happened to her mother.

"No."

It was the first she'd heard from the voice in a while. She wasn't sure she agreed with it, but thus far, it had been right. She sighed and kept quiet. For the time being.

The same could not be said for Eldon. He was still chattering about horses. Mags sighed as a feeling of comfort and connection washed over her. A little spark of something besides loneliness or guilt kindled inside of her. She let it and was content in the moment with her companions.

However, after about a block, and Eldon's long description of the horse he would buy, Mags sighed. "I think maybe we should consider an all-time gag policy."

The End

Acknowledgments

It takes a lot of people to make a book happen. First, thanks to Kevin Pettway. Thank you for allowing me to play in your sandbox. Second, the Mastermind, Kelly Colby. You are tough and supportive. Thank you for asking me to work on this project. Big thanks to my editor, Jesse. You are amazing to work with and you made this book go. Thanks to Shannon the Continuity Editor. You are straight-up incredible. Your pass on this book was like the delicious, grated cheese at the Olive Garden. I can give you no higher compliment.

I'd also like to thank Brigitte Nielsen. Why? Because I bet nobody has ever thanked her in a book before, but also because Red Sonja was one of my first loves in the world of sword and sorcery. I watched it at the perfect time as my fiction loving brain formed. I'm happy and grateful that I could add another fighting lady to the team.

About the Author

Jessica Raney grew up in the hills of southeastern Ohio looking for the Mothman and every other thing that goes bump in the dark Appalachian night. These days she resides in Houston, Texas and translates her love of Appalachia and dark things into stories that combine crime, fantasy, and horror into Appalachian Supernatural Noir. Her genre-blending series, *Tooth and Nail* showcases her love of all things creepy and quirky.

When not writing, she's navigating Houston traffic and enjoying the Gulf Coast with a weird little dog named Gimli.

Check out her website to sign up for her newsletter: www.jessicaraney.com.

CHECK OUT THE ANTHOLOGY FEATURING CHARACTERS FROM EACH MA SERIES

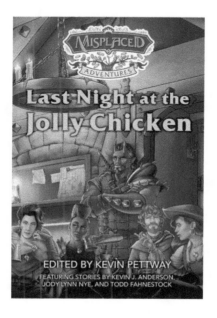

A card cursed with self-awareness seeks a hero to retrieve his creator from the afterlife. Nothing could possibly go wrong.

CHECK OUT THE SERIES THAT STARTED IT ALL

Stealing the cash box of your mercenary unit as you run away probably isn't wise, but it sure is funny.

CAN'T GET ENOUGH?
WE CAN'T EITHER.

What happens when you drag your magic-wielding siblings into a war they want nothing to do with? You get a family feud of epic proportions.

Printed in the USA
CPSIA information can be obtained
at www.ICGtesting.com
LVHW090615110924
790657LV00048B/516

9 781951 445522